ALEX'S
IRONCLAD RULES FOR LOVE

With additional comments by Dani

1. Women are a wise investment and should be chosen using that criterion. *Oh, spare me!*

2. Make sure she's an asset to your business and social standing. *Well, that lets me out!*

3. An heir is necessary. A brood is not. *But this "daddy" business gets addictive, doesn't it?*

4. A pliant woman is a ~~happy woman~~. *Barbie doll!*

5. Beware of smart women. *They'll know you too well.*

Dear Reader,

Are there really rules for falling in love?

You see them on the bookstands, hear about them on talk shows and discuss them with your friends. Rules for falling in love, or maybe more important, rules for helping someone fall in love with you! But can following the rules really make love happen?

My answer? I don't know. But I will tell you that in the past few months I've been blessed with finding a love of my own. Did I follow the rules? Some of them. Wouldn't you know that just like Sara and Matthew and Dani and Alex, I've had the same doubts, fears and joys of opening my heart to another. And just like them, I've found some age-old wisdom to be a great source of comfort: Be honest. Love unconditionally. Take the risk.

So, dear reader, as you read these stories I ask that you remember falling in love for the first time. Remember the advice that was given to you. And if you're so inclined, write to me and tell me about your Rules For Love. I'd love to share those moments and those memories with you.

Sincerely,

Jo Leigh
c/o Harlequin Books, 300 East 42nd Street,
New York, NY 10017.

Daddy 101

JO LEIGH

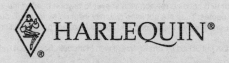

HARLEQUIN®

TORONTO • NEW YORK • LONDON
AMSTERDAM • PARIS • SYDNEY • HAMBURG
STOCKHOLM • ATHENS • TOKYO • MILAN • MADRID
PRAGUE • WARSAW • BUDAPEST • AUCKLAND

ISBN 0-373-16736-9

DADDY 101

Copyright © 1998 by Jolie Kramer.

Alexander Bradley's Ironclad Rules For Love:

1. Women are a wise investment and should be chosen using that criteria.
2. Make sure she's an asset to your business, to your social standing.
3. Beware of smart women.
4. Beauty may not last forever, but damn, it makes a big difference now.
5. Make sure she's content to shop, entertain, and not interfere.
6. An heir is necessary. A brood is not.
7. A pliant woman is a happy woman.
8. Don't get caught with your pants down.

Chapter One

"And would the Sexiest Man in the World care for a Danish with his coffee?"

"Knock it off, Ted."

"But it suits you so. I was thinking of having it embroidered on your towels for Christmas."

Alex Bradley grunted as he took the cheese Danish from the tray. "Go to hell, Ted. And don't forget to write."

"You have absolutely no sense of humor."

"I hired you, didn't I?"

"Touché."

"Can we get back to business now? I've got to leave in less than an hour."

Ted Chesterton, Alex's right-hand man, sat down across from his boss in his home office. All frivolity was gone now, and he had that worried frown that Alex enjoyed so much. It was one of the simple pleasures in his life to make Ted fret and stew. He was the best assistant Alex had ever had, but he was also alarmingly like a mother hen.

"Are you certain about this?" Ted asked.

"Yes. Next question."

"It's not too late to back out. People actually walk in New York. For blocks. Long blocks."

"You'll live."

Ted threw his hands up. "All right. I think you're crazy, but all right. I've put Pete's things in the car, including all his papers. They're in the glove box. So are your registration, and your maps."

"Okay. Now, about that Toronto mess…"

For the next twenty minutes, the conversation was strictly business as Alex made sure that every aspect of his company would be taken care of while he was on vacation. Of course, he would have the phone, the fax and the portable computer with him, and Ted would call constantly, but at least he wanted the illusion that he was leaving business behind for two weeks.

"I think that does it," Alex said finally. "Is there anything else?"

Ted scanned his notes quickly. "No. I think we'll muddle through somehow without you."

"I knew I could count on you. Now, I'm going to finish packing." Alex stood, and went over to pat Ted's shoulder. "You're a good man, Ted. No matter what everyone says."

"What?" He turned to follow Alex's progress out the door. "What who says? What are they saying?"

Alex waved goodbye and headed for his bedroom. Once there, he looked at the suitcase on the bed and saw that Ted or Patsy had refolded all his clothes so that they took up about half the space they once had. This seemed a bit much. He liked his personal staff, but did they have to treat him as if he were a ten-year-old just because he wanted to do something a little out of the ordinary?

The suitcase was one more reason he wanted to get the hell out of here and get on the road. Damn. A road trip. His first, he realized. He'd been across the country more times than he could count, but always by plane. This time, he was actually going to see some of this land of his. Stop at all the tourist traps and local diners and go to little country stores and hell, he might even see purple mountains' majesty and amber waves of grain.

He smiled as he went to gather his toiletries. He'd ordered a whole slew of books on cassette—unabridged, of course—for the trip. Books he'd meant to read, but never had. This was going to be a real vacation, a hiatus from all he knew. By the time he reached New York, Ted would have readied the new penthouse, and his regularly scheduled life would begin again. Only this time, on the East Coast.

Maybe, just maybe, this trip and the move would do the trick. Wake him up. Shake him out of this lethargy that had been weighing him down for so long. He sure as hell hoped so.

He studied his face in the mirror. It didn't hurt that he was leaving town just after that damned magazine had come out, either. He was the same old Alex. Good genes had given him the looks that had helped him so much in his life, but sexiest man in the world? If that were true, then the women of planet earth were in deep trouble. He might believe sexiest man on his block, but then he didn't know everyone who lived there.

He tucked his razor and his comb into his case and scanned the room briefly for anything he might have missed. Nope. He was ready. Once Pete was in the car, it was adios L.A., hello America. Alex Bradley was hitting the road.

Five days later

DANI JACOBSON tried hard to keep a cool, professional expression on her face. It would not do to laugh. Not now. This was a serious business. She lifted her stethoscope and placed it on the bunny's chest.

"Will he be okay?"

Dani listened intently, but heard nothing. Not that she'd expected to. But she went through the motions anyway. Finally she removed her stethoscope earpieces and looked at her patient's owner. "I think he's going to pull through."

Tiffany Cox sniffled once. "Thank you, Dr. Jacobson. Does he have to have a shot?"

Dani struggled once more to keep the smile from her lips and her voice. She nodded sagely at Tiffany, knowing the eight-year-old was legitimately concerned about Boppy, her stuffed bunny.

She went to the cabinet where she kept her syringes and took one down. "You don't have to watch if you don't want to, Tiffany."

"It's okay. I don't want Boppy to be scared."

"I'm glad you're here for him," Dani said as she took the empty syringe and placed it near the bunny's butt. "Are you two ready?"

Tiffany nodded. Boppy was elegantly blasé. She pushed the plunger. Tiffany winced.

In a second, it was over. "There. I think that's going to do the trick. But you take special care with Boppy now, you hear? No leaving him outside overnight."

The little blond girl scooped up the bunny and held him as if he were a baby. "No, ma'am. He'll get to sleep with me until he's all better."

"Excellent," Dani said, walking the girl to the examination room door. "I know he's in good hands." She heard Tiffany sniff once more as she went down the hallway toward the waiting room, where Dani knew five patients waited with real live animals that needed her attention. Oh well, it had only taken a moment. Surely no one would begrudge her that.

She went to the reception desk and picked up the case file on top of the stack. "Who's up next, Connie?" Dani read over the new patient form. An older dog having trouble breathing, but she didn't recognize the name. She turned over the page and saw that the owner was from out of town. Then she realized Connie hadn't answered her. Dani looked up. "Connie?"

Connie, her nineteen-year-old niece and receptionist, wasn't even looking her way. She was staring out into the waiting room. Not just staring, but slack-jawed staring. What kind of a dog was it?

Dani leaned forward and followed Connie's gaze. The dog was just a mutt. Nothing terribly special. Then she saw exactly what had caused Connie's stupefaction. It wasn't the dog. It was the owner. Holy cow. The man looked as if he'd just stepped off the cover of *GQ*. It wasn't only his dark good looks that had Connie drooling. Power radiated from this guy in almost visible waves. Power that was decidedly male, filled with testosterone and clearly designed to bring any female within a five-block radius to her knees.

Just the kind of man that Dani Jacobson couldn't stand.

She pulled back and looked once more at her niece's face. Only nineteen, and already besotted by good looks. "Connie," Dani said.

Connie didn't move.

"Connie!"

The young woman finally snapped out of her spell and turned. "Oh, be still my heart," she said. "You think he's single?"

Dani felt an old, terribly familiar anger blossom in the pit of her stomach. "It doesn't matter. When you see a man like him, you run. You don't stop to think. You don't entertain any notions. You leave and you don't look back."

Connie's eyes widened. "Are you serious?"

"Completely."

"Why?"

"Because any man who looks like that *knows* he looks like that."

"So?"

"Honey, in the sea of life, men like him are great white sharks. They don't think much, because they don't have to. They just feed, and mate with any available female. Trust me on this one."

Connie shook her head. "Sometimes you scare me, Dani," she said.

"Be that as it may, I don't want you speaking to that man, you hear? Just tell him to bring his dog to room three and that's it. When he leaves, ask for cash. Or a credit card. No checks. And whatever you do, don't look him in the eyes."

Her niece blinked a couple of times, then turned back to the shark. "Mr. Bradley," she said, her voice all quivery. "You can take Pete to room three."

Dani tucked the file under her arm and hurried back to her office. Mr. Bradley and Pete could wait a few minutes. As hard as it was to admit, her own heart was beating as fast as Connie's. It had to be because he looked so much like Randy. Or what Randy would look like in a few years. In that one brief glimpse out there, she'd felt as if she knew Mr. Bradley, which was impossible. But he sure did look familiar.

Her breathing and pulse rates were both back to normal, and she felt sure she could face the man without a problem. In the vernacular, she'd gotten a grip. And there was a dog out there who needed a doctor.

Absently running her hand over her short blond hair, Dani left the office and went right to room three. She stepped inside, and was caught off guard once more.

Mr. Bradley wasn't sitting in the chair where she expected him. He had gotten up on the metal examination table and was holding his big yellow dog in his lap.

"He's a little scared," he said. "He's not too crazy about doctors."

"I see," she said, wanting to tell him to leave the room, but knowing she couldn't. Not after looking into Pete's worried eyes.

"I'm Dr. Jacobson. I see in the chart that Pete has had some trouble breathing."

The man rubbed the dog's head with a tenderness that really surprised her. "He's an old guy," he said. "I'm not sure how old. He was at least two when I found him, and that was over ten years ago. Normally he likes to travel. But this time…" He looked at Dani. "I'm worried about him."

She should have shielded her eyes. Held her hands up to block his gaze. Anything would have been better than seeing that overwhelming compassion. Sharks don't feel compassion, right? Dani had always judged people by how they dealt with children and animals. She'd been surprised to see this guy with a dog in the first place. Now, as he sat in his slightly worn jeans and his pressed silk shirt, not worrying a bit that his old mutt was drooling— not on the jeans, but on the expensive material— she felt as though she wasn't on firm ground anymore.

The dog sneezed, which brought Dani out of her confusion. She made sure to look only at Pete as she walked up to the table. Holding out her hand to give the dog a chance to smell her, she took in the condition of his coat, his eyes, his tongue. "How you doing there, Pete? Hmm?" She petted the big yellow head, and Pete gave her a friendly nudge.

"I think he's okay for now, Mr. Bradley. I don't think he'll mind too much if you leave him to me. You can stay in the room if you like, but Pete and I have some things we need to do together. Isn't that right, Pete?"

"It's Alex, Dr. Jacobson," he said, then he lifted Pete's head so he could look the dog in the eyes. "You be good. I'll be right here, so don't worry." He petted the dog once more, then extricated himself from beneath him.

Dani kept her eyes on the dog until she heard the examination room door open. Her gaze moved there, surprised at the interruption. Normally, if there was something that needed her immediate attention, Connie buzzed her on the intercom. This time, Connie stood back so that she wasn't visible to Mr. Bradley. And she was holding a magazine in her hand.

Confused, Dani started to say something, but Connie waved furiously to abort that, and pointed to the picture on the cover of the magazine. Dani stared. Then she slowly turned her head to look at Alex Bradley, sitting calmly not two feet away. Holy mother of pearl, that's why he looked so familiar. She had the Sexiest Man in the World in examination room three!

Of course. Alex Bradley. Rich as sin and twice as handsome. The man who'd dated Cindy Crawford *and* Miss America. The media darling. The guy who was born with the silver spoon in his mouth. Who just happened to be terribly worried about an aging old mutt.

Dani looked once more at Connie. The young woman was holding the picture to her chest, practically swooning. Dani walked over to the door and closed it. Just because it was Alex Bradley, she couldn't forget her job or her position. Pete needed attention, and she would give it to him. Her pounding pulse was something she'd think about later. Right now, she had to keep her mind on Pete. Just Pete.

Alex watched the doctor's examination carefully. He was concerned about how good she could be. After all, this town was barely a flyspeck on the map. Carlson's Gap, New Mexico. The sign had said Population 18,000, but somehow, as he'd driven down the main street, he'd doubted the accuracy of that census. Maybe eighteen hundred. It didn't really matter. The vet had been in the phone book, and now Pete was being looked after. From what Alex could tell, the examination was pretty thorough, too.

His gaze moved from Pete to the doctor. The woman looked on the young side, maybe her late twenties. Her short blond hair was kind of tousled looking, and he didn't think she was wearing any makeup at all. Even so, or maybe because of that, she was very attractive. Not a great beauty by any stretch, but there was something sure and solid about her that Alex found appealing. Probably because sure and solid were two things on his forbidden list. The list his father had pounded into his head from the time he was ten years old.

Sure and solid were attributes that were not suitable. At least not for Alex. He was supposed to find someone a little timid and a little bit dim. Someone who could entertain at his parties, look good on his arm, not interfere. The only problem was that the women he was supposed to be attracted to never attracted him at all. Instead he was drawn to women like Dr. Dani Jacobson.

"Mr. Bradley?"

"Alex."

She didn't acknowledge his request. Instead she studied her chart. "Pete has a bronchial infection. His temperature is elevated and he's a little dehydrated. I'd like to keep him here for a few days and give him some antibiotics. Get that fever down."

"He's going to be okay, isn't he?" Alex stood and walked over to his old friend.

"If he's treated."

"Do whatever you need to," Alex said. "I don't want to lose this old guy. Not yet." He put his hand down and Pete nudged him until he found the spot behind his ear and scratched.

"I've given him a shot, and I'll take him to the back and set him up with an IV solution to take care of the dehydration. Why don't you come with me so I can show you where he'll be."

Alex nodded, then lifted Pete off the examination table and put him on the ground. Together, they followed the doctor out of the room and down the hall. They entered a spacious lab with quite a number of cages, several of them occupied. Pete started sniffing around, but Alex was just pleased to see everything looked clean and sanitary.

The receptionist walked in just then, and something must have spooked her, because she squealed.

"Connie, please help me set up a saline solution for Pete."

Connie responded with yet another little squeak. Alex saw her blush, and then he got it. It was that damn magazine. His guilty secret had been uncovered.

"Pete can stay in here."

Alex looked away from the young assistant to where the doctor stood. The cage was large, and there was a soft-looking pillow covering the floor. It was better than he'd expected.

"How long will he have to stay here?" Alex thought of Ted, and how delighted he was going to be when he found out Alex wasn't going to be in New York on schedule.

"Three days, if all goes well."

"I see. Well, fine. I just want him healthy. Can you point me to the nearest hotel?"

Dani finally looked up at him. He wondered briefly what she would look like with a smile on her face. Pretty, he'd bet. He did a quick survey of the rest of her. Despite the white lab coat, he could see she was quite trim. Petite. But there were curves there, too. Very nice, solid curves.

"I'm afraid we don't have a hotel here in town," she said. "The nearest one is about a hundred miles east."

"A hundred miles? I don't want to be that far from him."

"Dani has a room she rents out," the receptionist said. "You can stay with her."

"Connie!"

"Well, you do."

"I'm sure Mr. Bradley would rather stay at a hotel."

"No, it's okay. I really don't want to be so far from Pete. So if the room isn't rented..."

"It's not," Connie said quickly, ignoring the daggers the doctor was sending her. "It's comfortable, too."

He turned his attention to Dani once more. "I'd

be very grateful. Happy to pay whatever you think is fair.''

"I'm sorry, but I don't think—"

"Please," he said, stopping her objections. "If something should happen to Pete, and I wasn't here, I'd never forgive myself. So it's either the room, or I'm sleeping in the car. I'd prefer the room."

He could see the struggle on her face. It must have been the damn magazine that made her so hesitant. She probably thought the Sexiest Man in the World was also a sex fiend or something. "I'm perfectly safe," he said. "Completely housebroken."

That did it. He saw just the hint of a smile on her lips, and he knew the deal was done. And, he'd been right. She was prettier with a smile.

"All right," she said, looking first at Pete, then at him. "But I can't take you there now. We'll have to wait till I've seen the rest of my patients."

"Fine. Great. Whatever you say. Can I stay here and wait?"

She shook her head. "There's a diner across the street. I won't be too long. But we've got to get Pete settled."

He wasn't going to argue. He could use the time to notify Ted and pick up his E-mail. As long as he was close to Pete, it was all right with him. Three days in Carlson's Gap. Well, he'd wanted to see America. On the other hand, it was also two nights with Dani Jacobson. It might turn out to be an interesting side trip after all.

Chapter Two

Alex ordered a hamburger, french fries and a malt. It seemed appropriate fare in the old diner, with its long counter, plastic patched booths, and a tiny jukebox for each patron. Besides, he was on vacation. No baby Brie, no artichoke pâté for now. Just good old honest American food. He might even have a slice of pie for dessert.

He'd settled in the booth farthest from the door, anxious for some privacy. His laptop was open on the table, his briefcase beside him on the banquette and he'd just dialed Ted on the cellular. As the phone rang, he caught the waitress, a thin older woman with steel gray hair and thick glasses, staring at him. He must remember that the next time someone wanted to anoint him Sexiest Man in the World, he should say no.

Actually he'd not had a choice in the matter or he would have declined. But *World* magazine had decided his fate in some New York office sometime last winter. They'd neglected to tell him until one month before the issue arrived on the stands.

In the short time he'd been in the spotlight he'd come to recognize the signs that he'd been discovered. Wide-eyed, glassy stares. Pink cheeks and moistened lips. Actual pointing. Sometimes he got comments, mostly from men or older women, and he'd gotten a rather startling number of propositions from younger ladies. Many with photos attached. Keys, too. And of course there was that one memorable day when a busty blonde at the gym had asked him to autograph her left breast.

He had the feeling the waitress would not be asking him to sign any body parts, and for that he was grateful. However, he wished she would quit staring. It was damn hard to concentrate with gazes poking him, and he knew, also from experience, that once one person had recognized him, soon everyone in the immediate vicinity would feel the need to gape. Luckily the diner only had a few patrons and two other waitresses.

Ted answered the phone, and the staring was forgotten as Alex filled him in on his current situation. As predicted, Ted went ballistic when he found out about the delay. First, he wanted to send a jet to get Alex and Pete and fly them to New York. But Alex didn't want to move the old dog. Besides, he had no intention of cutting his trip short. Then Ted wanted to fly the Los Angeles vet out to Pete, but Alex put the kibosh on that plan, too. He had a good feeling about Dani Jacobson, and he'd learned to trust his instincts. Pete was in capable hands.

Ten minutes into the conversation, the waitress came back with his food. When Alex looked up to thank her, he saw that a few more tables were taken and the counter was getting crowded. But then Ted brought up Toronto, and Alex was instantly back to the matters at hand. He did, however, eat. He'd been right. It was an outstanding hamburger and the fries were damn good.

Soon the business with Ted was over, and Alex hung up. He didn't put the phone down, though. There were several matters that needed his personal attention, the first of which was calling his man in Canada. He dialed, then brought up a spreadsheet on his computer. It wasn't until the third ring that he noticed the quiet.

His stomach clenched and he felt a sudden chill. It was too quiet. There was no low murmur in the background, no orders being placed, no cash register jingle. Warily Alex raised his gaze.

The diner was packed. Every counter seat, every booth, every table occupied. Maybe twenty people stood by the back wall. And every pair of eyes was focused on him.

He was vaguely aware that someone on the phone said hello. His thumb moved to the disconnect button and he pressed it. The line needed to be clear for his call to 911.

What had he stumbled into? All he could think

of was that old movie *The Birds*. That's what they
looked like. The ravens and the finches lined up on
the rooftops and the phone wires. At any moment,
Alex expected to see Hitchcock himself. No one
spoke. No one moved. They all just stared at him
as though he were an exhibit...or a target.

He slowly, very slowly, moved his arm down.
The gazes of a hundred people followed that arm
until it was hidden below the table. Then, as one,
the stares shifted back to his face. He leaned to his
right, just to see. Sure enough, everyone there
moved with him. All of them leaned just a bit. He
straightened. They straightened. The theme music
from the ''Twilight Zone'' echoed in his head.

If he got up and walked outside, would they follow? Or would they stop him before he cleared the
door? Why wasn't anyone blinking, for God's
sake?

Just then, the door to the diner opened. No one
bothered to look. They all just kept staring at him.
He risked it, though. He turned his gaze to the door
and saw that it was Dani. He instantly felt relieved.
Until she stopped. Turned. Stared. For one crazy
moment, he pictured her leading the charge. Shouting, ''Get him!'' and the whole damn crowd lung-
ing forward. But then...

''Oh, for heaven's sake,'' she said, her voice cutting through the silence as if it were a heavy blade.
''Don't you people have better things to do with
your time?''

She put her hands on her hips, and let her gaze rake the crowd. "Stephanie, you get back to school this instant. Francine, who's watching the store? Terry, you should know better. I swear, you probably scared the poor man to death."

That was it. Someone stood. A woman laughed. The cook dinged his bell. Alex breathed again.

Dani hustled a few more folks to their feet, then came over to his booth. She sat down across from him, a scowl making her lovely face somehow lovelier. He'd never been so happy to see anyone in his life.

"Sorry about that," she said.

"I thought I was a goner."

"They don't mean any harm. We just don't get many celebrities here."

"So you know about the magazine?"

She nodded. Then her gaze moved quickly from his face to his plate. "Why'd you do it?" she asked, her focus entirely on his leftover fries.

He took advantage of her shifted interest to study her clear, perfect skin. Her long lashes. Her full pink lips. "What?"

"Get yourself in that silly magazine?"

"I didn't volunteer. I was drafted."

She nodded, giving him a quick glance. But the draw of the fries was obviously too much for her. He shoved the plate across the table. "Go ahead."

She frowned. "Go ahead?"

"The fries. I'm done."

She looked at him quizzically. "I'm happy for you."

"Don't you want them?"

"Your fries?"

"Yes."

"No."

"Well then, why have you been staring at them?"

"I haven't."

"Yes, you have."

"I would know if I were staring at fries."

"If you weren't staring at the fries, what were you staring at?"

"I wasn't staring *at* anything. I just wasn't staring at you."

"Oh," he said, more confused than ever. Then he noticed her cheeks flush pink. "Oh," he said, the light dawning. It was the magazine again. The celebrity business. "It's all hype, Dani. No big deal."

"What's all hype?"

"We're not going to start this again, are we?"

"Start what?"

He smiled. He shouldn't have. She was clearly flustered. A gentleman would let it drop, let her gather her composure. But he was no gentleman. "I'm not really the Sexiest Man in the World," he said, lowering his voice as he leaned forward. "I'm just a man. A regular, ordinary man. But if you like,

I promise to be as sexy as I can while I'm staying with you.''

Her cheeks changed from pink to a rather fetching red. But then he captured her gaze, and the cheeks were forgotten. Those blue eyes showed him her nervousness, her hesitation. And, what do you know, her excitement.

The seconds ticked by. He didn't let go of her gaze, but held her steady. Her emotions were unguarded, and as he watched, her nervousness ebbed and the hint of excitement grew. Not much, but enough.

"What?" she asked softly.

"I said I'll do my best to live up to my image."

The cook's bell dinged, and she ripped her gaze away. She sat back in the booth and crossed her arms over her chest. "We are *not* going there. Understand? Not now. Not when you're a guest in my home. Not even for a second."

It was his turn to lean back. He'd thought he was fanning an ember, when it was clear he'd lit a bonfire.

Her eyes narrowed and a new flush of pink tinged her cheeks. But this time it wasn't from embarrassment or awareness. This was anger, pure and simple. "I know you think you can get any woman by crooking your little finger, buster, but not here. No, sir. I've seen your kind before. Just because you're rich and handsome doesn't mean you can run roughshod over people's lives. There are repercussions, you know. People have feelings. You don't just waltz in here, mess everything up and waltz out again." She slid out of the booth and stood, moving her hands to her hips. "Do you want me to show you your room or not?"

Alex blinked. "Yes, I do."

"Well, then?"

"Let me pay my bill," he said, trying to find his equilibrium. What the hell was he getting himself into? This woman might be a competent vet, but she was clearly nuts. He went for his wallet, trying hard to think of what he'd done to warrant the wrath of Dani. It wasn't as if he'd grabbed her or anything. Okay, so he shouldn't have made that comment. But a man's got to try, right?

He heard a small impatient sigh, and when he looked at her once more he could tell she was just itching to go. He left a couple of dollars on the table, picked up the tab and stood. Right next to her. The top of her head came just to the tip of his chin. She had to look up to meet his gaze. When she did, he thought about smiling. About cutting the tension that arced between them. But it was immediately clear a smile would not have the desired effect. She was out for bear, and he was Smokey.

"Oh, I'll wait outside," she said, turning abruptly.

All Alex could do was watch her go. She stomped her way across the diner, then pulled the door open with surprising vigor. He just stood there, watching the door slowly close, wondering what in the hell had just happened.

"Don't mind her, hon."

He turned to see the older waitress at his elbow.

"She's a good girl. But she's got her notions."

"I see," Alex said, even though he didn't.

"You just don't let this bother you. She'll get over it. She always does."

"You mean this has happened before?"

The older woman nodded. "Yep. Haven't seen her this bad in a while though."

"I feel like I should apologize. But I don't know for what."

The waitress laughed. "That sounds about right. Don't worry about it. She's just being Dani. Been like that since she was a baby."

"You've known her a long time?"

"I hope so. I'm her mother."

"Her what?"

"I'm Phyllis Jacobson. My husband Dooley is back there cooking. This is our place."

He turned to face her. "I'm Alex Bradley. My dog is—"

"I know," she said. "Your dog is sick and Dani's caring for him. You're staying out at her place."

"How?"

"You haven't lived in a small town, have you?"

He shook his head.

"Honey, out here, somebody itches and we all scratch."

"So tell me, Mrs. Jacobson. What did I do wrong?"

She laughed again, and he could see where Dani got her smile. Now that he looked, there was a family resemblance. Even through the thick glasses the older woman's eyes were almost as blue as her daughter's. And as intelligent.

"You were born a handsome man. Made yourself a success. Got yourself some money. Nothing you can do about any of those things that I can see."

"Ah. So if I was ugly, unemployed and broke, I'd be welcomed with open arms?"

Mrs. Jacobson shrugged. "Might be. But you go on now. Don't make her stand out there by herself. It'll just get worse."

"Worse?"

"You haven't seen anything yet."

"Maybe I should just sleep in my car."

The woman eyed him from his shoes to his forehead. "You don't seem the type of man who avoids trouble when it calls."

"And she's trouble."

"That she is. But she's worth it."

He crooked his brow. "Oh?"

The woman reached over and took the bill from his hand. "It's on the house, this time," she said, then she met his gaze squarely. "She's worth it all right, but you aren't gonna be around long enough to see that. So just be nice, don't take it personally and everything will work out fine.''

He stared back for a long while. ''Why do I feel like I've just been given a warning?''

'''Cause you're a smart man. You hurt that girl, you'll have a whole town to deal with.''

''I see.''

''No, you don't. But mess with our Dani, and you will.''

THE DRIVE TO DANI'S PLACE didn't lighten her mood. She'd wanted to walk, but he'd convinced her to accompany him in his car. When she'd seen the black Mercedes, she'd scowled at him, and the scowl deepened as she saw the plush leather interior, the fax machine and the cellular phone. She'd spoken as little as possible, and he thought it best not to push.

He stopped the car in front of a small two-story Victorian house, white with blue trim. The yard was neat, the house well kept. Dani was out the door the moment he came to a full stop. She walked up the small path, and turned to wait for him. Impatiently of course.

He took his time. What he couldn't figure out was why her behavior wasn't making him angry. There was no sugarcoating the fact that she was rude, belligerent and completely unreasonable. He should have been steaming by now. Instead he was intrigued. And a little aroused. That was the most troubling thing. Sure, she was attractive in her own way, but not enough to warrant his current state of discomfort. Physical beauty was something he was used to. It was nice, but it wasn't enough, on its own, to turn him on. And frankly he'd been with women a lot more beautiful than Dani. So what was it?

He got his suitcase from the trunk and slammed the lid down. As he walked up the path, he studied his hostess. She was clearly not his type. Nothing about her said demure. He couldn't imagine her smiling benignly at a cocktail party, or quietly excusing herself when talk turned to business. No, she had none of the traits he was after. She was wrong, wrong, wrong.

And he wanted her.

There was no use denying the fact that just watching her, even now when she looked flustered and angry, was enough to get him half hard. Damn.

She swung the front door open and walked in, not waiting for him to even reach the front stoop. He followed. The first thing he noticed was the artwork. Finger painting. On the wall. Directly. No canvas. It was actually pretty good.

Dani noticed it, too. She took a deep breath, looked up the staircase and called, ''Chloe Jacobson, you get your little butt down here right this minute!''

Behind him, Alex heard a snuffle, and he turned

toward the living room. There was an elderly woman stretched out on the couch, just stirring from a nap. Then he heard stomping, and he turned back to the stairs.

He saw a perfectly beautiful little girl coming down to join them. The green paint on her face, in her hair and on her hands did little to mask her prettiness. She looked just like a younger version of Dani.

"What's this?" Dani said, pointing to the painting.

"It's a landscape," the girl said.

"Why is it on the wall?"

Chloe shook her head slowly. "It's a mural. They're supposed to be on the wall."

"Don't you think you should have asked permission before you painted a mural on my wall?"

"You would have said no." The girl reached the landing and stared up at Alex. He'd originally thought she was very young. Seven or eight. But after that bit of conversation, he revised his estimate. Maybe she was just little for her age.

"Who are you?" she asked.

"I'm Alex Bradley," he said, a bit unnerved by her inquisitive gaze. He wasn't used to kids.

"He's a guest," Dani said. "He'll be here for a day or so."

"Why?" Chloe asked.

"Because I'm taking care of his dog." Dani went

over to the masterpiece on the wall and touched the paint. "It's dry."

"Not completely," Chloe said, dismissing him. "So be careful."

"It's not going to stay here," Dani said.

"Why not? You're always encouraging me to express myself."

"Chloe." The word was drawn out, with a slight upturn at the end. It signaled trouble, and Alex wasn't the only one to notice.

"Oh, all right. But honestly, Mother. You can be so narrow-minded sometimes."

Alex heard a gasp from the living room. The woman on the couch was up now, and she'd seen the mural. "Oh, heavens. Chloe, what did you do?"

Chloe looked at the woman with highly intelligent and somewhat devilish eyes. "I tried to bring a little culture into the house, that's all."

"It's all right, Mimi," Dani said. "You can go on home. Ralph is waiting on his dinner. Thanks for watching her."

"But—"

"Chloe's going to clean it all up. Aren't you, Chloe?"

With a dramatic sigh, Chloe crossed her green spattered arms over her chest in a gesture that was pure Dani. Mimi collected her things and after a long look at Alex, then another long look at Dani, shook her head and left.

Dani turned toward Chloe. "While you're at it, clean yourself up, too. You look like a leprechaun."

Alex heard the little girl snort before she headed toward the back of the house.

Dani turned to him, her exasperation evident. At least she wasn't still angry at him. "That was my daughter."

"Interesting kid," he said.

"You have no idea." Dani shook her head. "She's eight. Eight. I'm just *so* looking forward to her teenage years!"

"She seems awfully sophisticated," he said.

"That's one way of putting it. Chloe is gifted. She's also clever, manipulative and whatever you do, don't play cards with her."

"No?"

Dani shook her head. "The last person who played with Chloe lost a hundred and forty-two dollars."

"Wow."

"She counts cards."

"I see."

"And cheats."

"Uh-huh."

"So just be careful."

"Okay."

"And quit looking at me like that."

"Like what?"

"Like that. With those eyes."

"They're the only eyes I have."

"You know what I mean."

He almost denied it. But he did know what she meant. What he didn't know was if he could stop. She was just so damn…something. There was the kicker. He didn't know what she was. Or why he couldn't keep his equilibrium around her. "Maybe I should just go to my room."

She nodded. "Right. Follow me."

Dani led him to the staircase, and he was treated to the lovely and evocative view of her behind as she walked up. Even though she was quite petite, her derrière flared nicely from her small waist. He wanted the stairs to go on quite a bit farther than they did.

Once they were on the second floor, she walked him past two rooms, one clearly Chloe's bedroom, and a bathroom. Then she opened up a third door and waited for him to enter.

The room was small, but comfortable. A queen-size bed was the centerpiece. A dresser, a nightstand and a television comprised the rest of the decor. The built-in bookcases on the right wall were full, and she had a Chagall print above the bed. Everything looked right, and neat and none of it felt like Dani.

"There are fresh towels in the bathroom," she said. "If you need anything else, let me know."

He walked to the bed and put his suitcase down. When he turned, she was still at the door. "Thank you," he said. "I know this is inconvenient for you. I promise I'll stay out of your hair."

She stared at him a minute more, then he heard her sigh. "I'm sorry. I shouldn't have gotten so bent out of shape."

"It's okay. It happens."

"It didn't need to happen with you," she said. "I've been a little edgy lately, is all."

He moved toward her, and he saw her hand tighten on the doorknob. "It's very nice of you to let me hang around. For Pete's sake, I mean."

"He's going to be fine," she said, her gaze locked on to his.

He took another step, watching to see if she'd back up. She didn't.

"You can come see him tomorrow," she said, her voice just a tiny bit shaky.

He was very close to her now. Close enough to take her into his arms. To kiss her. To run his hands down her back and cup her derrière. But he didn't. At least he was sane enough to realize his thoughts were completely out of line. They'd just met. She didn't like him very much. He was a guest in her home. But, damn, he wanted to taste that mouth. The mouth that opened slightly. The lips she moistened with the tip of her pink tongue. But he didn't. He didn't.

She did.

Chapter Three

Dani leaned forward. It wasn't a voluntary motion. Something pulled her from the front, pushed her from the back. If she kept going, her lips would meet his.

Her eyes widened as she inched toward him. She could see the surprise in his gaze, the slow smile. She willed herself to stop just as she raised on tiptoes. If he leaned forward a fraction of an inch, they would kiss. If she moved even a smidgen, it would happen.

Then the unseen hands released her. Her sanity rushed back with a thud as she quickly moved backward. Heat filled more than her cheeks. Her whole face, her neck, even her hands were infused with hot humiliation.

"I'd better unpack," he said, his voice low and husky.

"Uh-huh," she said, her eloquence only matched by her mature demeanor. She could only be grateful, immeasurably grateful, that he had the good taste not to bring up her momentary lapse.

She stepped farther back, closing his door, wanting to get the heck away from Alex Bradley and his lips.

"But I will want that kiss," he said. "Later."

She slammed the door shut and buried her head in her hands. What in hell had she been thinking? Was she nuts? She'd almost kissed a stranger. A rich, powerful, handsome stranger who was a guest in her home. A man she seriously disliked on general principles. A man she knew better than to talk to, let alone kiss, because she knew all too well that kind of man was nothing but trouble. She couldn't let him think…

She turned abruptly and opened the door once more. Alex stood by the bed, boxer shorts in one hand, a pair of socks in the other.

"I won't," she said.

"Won't what?"

"Kiss you."

"Okay."

She slammed the door again, and this time, she walked away. Her confusion, however, didn't lessen. What had come over her? She wasn't prone to flights of fancy. Or acting on whims. She was sensible…some said to a fault. But her good sense and her no-nonsense approach to life were the very things that had helped her get to this point in her life. She had the career she wanted, she owned her home, and of course there was Chloe.

Hormones. It had to be hormones running amok. He had pheromones, didn't he? She obviously was just responding to some primitive smell. That wasn't her fault. She couldn't help it if some part of her brain decided to react to his scent.

Dani hurried down the stairs and went right to her bedroom. On her dresser were several bottles of perfume and lotion. She wasn't exactly a perfume kind of woman, but this was an emergency. She took the strongest scent she had, Opium, and put a dab behind each ear, then, just for safety's sake, she put a small drop just below her nose. The heady aroma blocked most anything else, and she instantly felt more relaxed. Let his pheromones try to get past this!

Feeling much more at ease, Dani left the bedroom and headed for the kitchen. Chloe was there ahead of her, sitting at the table with her pale green hands folded. Dani sighed. It wasn't the first time her little darling had turned colors. Just the latest.

"Who is that man, Mommy?"

"He's just a guest. I'm taking care of his dog at the clinic."

"Why is he staying here? I thought you said you weren't going to have guests here anymore. That you didn't have to now that the clinic was starting to pay off and that the last thing you needed was to worry about some stranger walking off with your jewelry or worse?''

Dani got the hamburger package from the fridge and put it on the counter. ''Did you clean off the wall?''

''Mostly. When did you meet him?''

''What do you mean, mostly?''

''Some of it is a little hard to get off. Why are you breaking the rules?''

Dani got a big bowl from the cupboard and started preparing the meat loaf. She broke a couple of eggs so hard, large pieces of shell fell in and she had to dig them out. ''Quit changing the subject, Chloe. I expect that wall to be pristine. You know what pristine means?''

''Clean,'' Chloe said impatiently. ''You're the one changing the subject.''

Dani turned to her with her best ''Mom's getting fed up'' look. ''The man's name is Mr. Bradley. He's only here for a couple of days, until his dog gets well. It's not breaking any rules, and besides, they're my rules, and if I want to break them, I can.''

Chloe frowned. ''Do I have to be nice to him?''

''Of course you do.''

''But he's only going to be here a couple of days, right?''

''Even if he was only here ten minutes, you'd have to be nice to him.''

''Well, I don't like him.''

"Why not?"

"Because."

"That's no reason."

Chloe's right brow lifted. "You use it all the time."

Once again, Dani realized that having a kid whose IQ was 180 wasn't for sissies. Her lovely green daughter remembered everything. Every conversation. Every mistake. "That's a mother's prerogative," she said.

"But that's not fair."

"We've talked about fair before, haven't we?"

Chloe stood up, and Dani saw that although she'd tried to wash the green paint from her skin, she'd only managed to spread the color to her dress, her upper arms and somehow even her legs.

"The world isn't a fair place," Chloe said, repeating verbatim a conversation that had taken place over two years before. "I might as well get used to the idea."

"That's right."

"It still sucks."

"Chloe!"

"What? That's not a curse word."

"It's close enough."

The little girl looked at her with eyes too old and wise for one so young. "I think you asked him to stay here because he looks like a movie star."

"What?"

"He looks like that guy you're always sighing over. Harrison Ford."

"He does not."

"Yes, he does."

"He... It doesn't matter," Dani said, turning back to the meat loaf. "Now go get in the tub, and put that dress into the hamper."

"I thought you wanted the wall to be pristine?"

"Chloe. Just go."

"Mothers," Chloe muttered as she walked slowly out of the room. "I'll never understand them."

Dani couldn't help but smile. Despite the annoyance of having her own words come back to haunt her time and time again, she wouldn't trade her little genius for any other kid in the world. Although it would be nice, every once in a while, to slip an easy answer into the mix. To have Chloe look at her with silent awed devotion instead of the quizzical cynicism that had been there since Chloe had learned to talk.

Dani's hands plunged into the gooey mess of raw beef, egg and bread crumbs. As she worked, she thought about what Chloe had said. The Harrison Ford remark. It was true Alex did have dark hair, he was tall and well built, and he had those great lines bracketing his mouth that seemed to add such character to his already handsome face. But Harrison Ford? Please. Well, okay. Maybe in *Patriot Games*. But certainly not *Witness*.

She mixed the hamburger for a few more minutes, thinking all the while of the kiss in *Witness*, the one that was so desperate, so passionate that it fairly leapt off the screen. That was one of her favorite film moments and it never failed to make her squirm just a bit in her seat. Which was a very good reason not to think about it now. Not with *him* upstairs.

Being the sensible woman she was, she completely stopped thinking about kisses and movie stars and the man upstairs and concentrated on finishing dinner. Well, almost completely.

ALEX SURVEYED the small room with a critical eye. It was approximately the size of his closet back home, but it had all the necessary equipment, especially now that he'd set up his computer, fax, printer and cell phone. He could conduct business here as easily as at a hotel, if, that is, he could focus. The distraction level here in Dani's house was high. The sounds were different from hotel sounds, the ambience less anonymous. And, of course, there was Dani.

His thoughts hadn't wandered far from that topic even though he'd made a conscious effort to do so. It was clear she found him somewhat appealing. Just as clear that she didn't want to find him appealing at all. He wondered, not for the first time, if she had her own set of rules she lived by. Had her mother told her time and time again not to get involved with a man like him? Did she have a checklist, not written on paper but ingrained in her so solidly that each decision was based on a stringent code she'd memorized?

The thought wasn't a comfort, even though he completely understood. Certainly Dani didn't know him well enough to dislike him based on his personality. It had to have been some outside trigger that made her so prickly around him. This wasn't the first time a woman had given him clear signals to leave her be, but this was different. Dani wasn't intimidated by him. On the contrary. The "almost" kiss had shown him she found something about him compelling. But it hadn't changed the fact that she didn't like him. No, that's not it. That she didn't *want* to like him. What did he represent to her?

The question had been rolling around in his brain for the last hour. Somehow, he had to get the answer. Why it was so important wasn't terribly clear. Maybe he was just bored. Or curious. Or maybe he wanted to change her mind.

He sat down at the dresser he'd converted to a desktop. It wasn't comfortable, no place to put his legs, but serviceable. He needed to get online to fetch his E-mail, but there was only one phone hookup in the room. He didn't want to tie up Dani's only line.

He heard a soft tap at the door. "Come in."

The door came open slowly. Dani stepped inside. She caught sight of his impromptu desk as he stood.

"I hope you don't mind," he said. "I see you only have one line and I don't want to tie it up."

She shrugged. "I've got a private line for work calls. It's fine."

"I'll pay for any long-distance charges."

"I know."

He smiled. "Would you like that in cash, up front?"

She smiled back at him. "I know where to find you if you try to skip town."

This was nice. This Dani with her easy smile and gentle humor.

"Dinner's ready," she said. "Downstairs."

"Great."

"And I called the clinic. Pete's doing fine. If you like, we can go over to see him after dinner."

"I'd like that a lot."

Her gaze finally rested on his. He wondered what had happened to change her mood. Her eyes were wide and unguarded, friendly. Something had shifted. But what?

"Well," she said, a slight flush coloring her cheek. "There are fresh towels in the bathroom, if you want to wash up."

"Thanks."

"I hope you like meat loaf and mashed potatoes."

"Love 'em."

"Good. Okay. Well…"

"I'll go get ready."

She looked at him for a few more seconds, then turned away abruptly. "Take your time," she said, pulling the door closed behind her.

Alex shook his head. He didn't get it. He'd never had trouble talking to a woman. Not since the onset of puberty at least. But with Dani, it seemed that there were two conversations going on at once. One was mundane and a little stilted. The other was silent, and rife with tension. It was the silent communication that had him intrigued. What did she see when she looked at him that way? And why in hell did he care so much?

DANI HURRIED DOWN the stairs. She found it hard to believe that just having a male body in the house was so disconcerting. Darn those pesky hormones. They certainly were persistent little rascals. Even during that brief and completely harmless conversation, she'd been aware of her rapid pulse, the heat in her flesh, the clench in her tummy. All signs of sexual arousal, which, although inconvenient and slightly embarrassing, were as natural and as meaningful as a hiccup.

It really had nothing to do with Alex himself. He could have been any guy she wanted to sleep with.

She stopped short, just shy of the kitchen. That last thought had been backward. It was biology that made her think of sex with Alex. Not her interest in him that kicked her hormones into gear. Very important distinction.

"Why are you standing there?"

Chloe's voice startled her and she realized her daughter was standing only a few feet away. Her long blond hair was wet from her bath, but combed neatly. Instead of the green painted dress, she wore her white frilly nightgown, the one she saved for special occasions. There was still a hint of green on her arms, but Dani figured one more good bath and that would be gone.

"I thought dinner was ready," Chloe said. "Is he going to eat with us? I saw three places set at the table. What are we going to talk about? Do I really have to be nice?"

Dani continued walking into the kitchen, confident that Chloe would keep up with her. There were unanswered questions in the room, and Chloe couldn't stand an unanswered question.

"Please pour the water, Chloe, and put the salad dressing on the table."

"But—"

Dani turned to her daughter, amazed as always that she was already so tall at eight. Of course her father was six foot four. "Dinner is ready. Mr. Bradley is going to eat with us. We'll talk about whatever he wants, because he's our guest. And yes, you really do have to be nice."

"I appreciate the being nice part," Alex said, rounding the corner. "But we don't have to talk about what I want to. As a matter of fact, I've been awfully curious to find out more about that mural."

Chloe spun around as Dani tried to calm her heart. He'd surprised her, that's all. Nothing more.

"You don't care about the mural," Chloe said. "You're just trying to be nice to me, aren't you?"

"Hmm." Alex studied the girl and Dani could see he was struggling not to smile. "Nope. I really hadn't thought about being nice. But I will if you like."

Chloe crossed her arms over her chest. "You needn't bother. We won't know each other long enough for it to matter."

Alex looked at Dani. "Needn't bother?"

It was Dani's turn to grin.

"It's proper English," Chloe said, her voice holding just a hint of a worried question.

"That's right," Dani said. "It is."

"I see I'm going to have to be on my toes around here, aren't I?" Alex said. "Watch my split infinitives. But I am still interested in the mural, regardless of the length of our acquaintance."

Chloe's arms dropped and she turned toward the fridge. "I just thought a mural would be nice there. That's all." She got the water pitcher and walked to the table. She filled each of the three glasses, concentrating hard.

"Are you interested in other forms of art?" Alex asked.

Dani didn't hear any condescension in his voice. Either he was a very good actor, or he was actually curious. She hoped for the latter, but expected it was the former. "Please sit down, Mr. Bradley. Everything's ready."

Chloe put the water back and brought out three bottles of salad dressing and placed them in the center of the table. Then she sat down. "I'm interested in all forms of art," she said, sounding like the thirty-year-old her mother suspected was trapped inside the little girl's body.

"I am, too," Alex said. "I have a small collection of original pieces at my place. Maybe sometime you'll come out and see them."

"Where is your place?"

"New York. At least it will be in about a week."

Dani brought the meat loaf to the table and got busy serving. She was grateful that Chloe was carrying the conversation. It was much easier being a spectator than a player. At least with Alex.

"What kind of a collection?" Chloe asked.

"It's pretty eclectic. I've got a small Rubens, and a couple of Andy Warhol soup cans. A few other modern painters, but mostly I've concentrated on the French Impressionists."

"Mom has a Monet print in her bedroom."

Dani looked up just in time to see Alex react to the fact that Chloe knew about the French Impressionists. How she knew, Dani didn't know. But after living with her for eight years, Dani had just learned to accept her little genius for what she was.

"I see," Alex said, keeping the shock from his voice quite admirably. "Do you like it?"

"It's okay. I like the Hopper in her office better."

"Hopper," he said, almost to himself. "*Night Hawks,* right?"

Chloe smiled. A genuine smile. An approving smile. "You know him?"

"I do."

"You like him?"

"I've got two lithographs of his."

Chloe nodded, then turned to Dani. "When can we go to New York?"

Dani laughed as she sat down. "Not this evening. You have homework."

"I'm not joking, Mother. I want to go see his collection. He invited me." She turned to Alex. "Didn't you?"

Alex nodded. "I invited both of you. You're welcome anytime."

Chloe stared at Dani once more. "Well?"

"We'll discuss it later. Eat your meat loaf."

"It's very good," Alex said.

Dani saw he'd already eaten a good portion of the meat, as well as the mashed potatoes, the green beans and his salad. It had been a long time since she'd had a man over for dinner. A healthy, active man, that is. With a healthy man's appetite. "Thank you. There's more, when you're ready."

"I don't get a lot of meat loaf at home," he said. "Don't know why."

"You don't cook for yourself, do you?"

He shook his head. "It's a good thing, too. I'm hopeless in the kitchen."

"I'll bet you've never tried. Never had to, right?"

"No, I never have."

She knew he was looking at her, waiting to catch her gaze. She wasn't being nice. It wasn't his fault he'd been born with a silver spoon in his mouth. But dammit, she had no patience for people who couldn't take care of themselves.

The doorbell rang, giving her a perfect excuse to get up from the table. "Excuse me," she said, although she should have said, "I'm sorry." Hadn't she just told Chloe to be nice to the guest?

She walked to the front door and opened it. Caroline Tully, a woman Dani hardly knew, stood in front of her. She was dressed to the nines in a tight red dress, high heels and enough makeup to last for days. She also held a casserole dish in her hands.

"Hi, Dani," Caroline said, peering over her shoulder.

"Hello."

Caroline finally glanced at her. "Is he here?" she asked, her whisper conspiratorial.

"Who?" Dani asked, although she knew perfectly well.

"Him. Alex Bradley. I heard about it this afternoon. I can't believe it. Where is he?" Not waiting for an invitation, Caroline stepped inside, brushing past Dani. "I just thought, well, with you being busy at the clinic and all..."

Dani closed the door and followed her unexpected visitor to the kitchen. She had to slow as Caroline spotted her prey.

"I just thought that I'd bring over this little old dinner. In case, you know. That you didn't have time for cooking, what with you working so hard and all."

"Thanks for the thought," Dani said, trying hard to control her temper.

Caroline stood still, staring at Alex Bradley and pushing out her cleavage.

Alex stood up, smiling.

"Aren't you going to introduce us?" Caroline whispered in a pseudo-Marilyn Monroe breathy tone that made Dani want to pinch her.

"Alex Bradley, Caroline Tully."

"How do you do?" Alex said.

Caroline giggled. Dani sighed. She should have been prepared for this. The women of this town were never going to let an opportunity like this get past them. Caroline might be the first, but she certainly wasn't going to be the last. Dani might not have to cook again for six months. They were all going to be dressed up. Wearing makeup and tight dresses. Showing off their bonded teeth, their feminine giggles. Every one of them hoping against hope that the Sexiest Man in the World would get one look at them and never want to leave.

They didn't get it. Never would, probably. There was nothing and no one in this little town that would make a man like Alex Bradley stay. Nothing at all to keep him here. He'd leave. Oh, yes. He'd leave.

Chapter Four

Alex sized up Caroline Tully in five hot seconds.
Single, probably divorced. No kids, but the biological clock ticking away. Dated the popular boys, but
married the one with potential. Left him when his
job dead-ended. Looking for a mate.

Of course he couldn't ask her how much of his
prognostication was correct, but maybe Dani would
tell him later. His gaze switched to his hostess. She
was scowling at her visitor. Interesting. Was it because Caroline just dropped by, or because she'd
dropped by to see him?

"I read the article about you in the *World*," Caroline said. Her voice was all wispy, as if she'd had
a serious case of TB at some point.

"I plead the Fifth," he said. "I take no respon-
sibility for their exaggerations."

Caroline took a step forward. "I see now they
didn't do you justice."

Alex had to struggle not to roll his eyes. He

looked at Chloe as a diversionary tactic, and *she* rolled her eyes. It was difficult not to laugh.

"I hope you like mango and lime glazed Cornish hens," Caroline said.

"It sounds wonderful," Alex said, clicking back into polite mode. He reached for the casserole dish. "Let me take that from you."

As he took it, he felt two fingers, one from each hand, brush his. But instead of reacting to the very overt sexual ploy, he thought immediately about another touch. His gaze moved back to Dani. With her touch, he'd crackled like a live wire. Caroline's was just a dead end.

However, he'd not been raised by wolves, and as he put the food down, he held his chair for the guest. "Care to join us?"

"Actually," Dani said, stopping Caroline before she could get a word out. "We were just finishing here, and I promised to take Alex to the clinic." Dani moved close to Caroline, and put a friendly arm around her shoulder. She hooked the taller woman in a semicircle and started her toward the door.

"But—" Caroline turned her head to look back at Alex.

"Very nice meeting you," Alex said. "And thanks for the chicken."

They were already at the door, and Dani had it open. She didn't exactly shove Caroline out, but she didn't pussyfoot around, either. In two shakes, the door was swinging closed. Alex heard Caroline call out, "Cornish game..." and then she was gone.

When Dani turned, the scowl had been replaced by a very satisfied smile. She walked back, her step just a little bit jaunty.

"Your best friend?" Alex asked.

"Hardly. I've barely said two words to her."

"But she went to so much trouble for you."

"For me? Come now, Alex. Don't be coy."

"Me? Coy? Never."

Dani took her seat again and Alex followed suit.

"This isn't going to be the last time someone drops by, you know," she said.

"That seems quite neighborly."

"Ha! There are quite a few single women in this town, Alex. And each and every one of them is at this moment frantically going through her collection of Martha Stewart recipes trying to figure out what would impress a man like you. Mango and lime glazed hens. Sheesh."

He didn't say anything for a moment. He just watched her. She was jealous. Nothing life threatening, but it was there. He'd like to think it was because of their almost-kiss. Because of the electric touch. But he wasn't a hundred percent convinced. It might just be territorial, and not personal. Time to make sure. He held out his plate. "I think I will have some more of that meat loaf." She took the dish and served him another piece. As she passed it back, he made sure his fingers touched hers.

Whammo. Another lightning bolt. He felt it all the way down to his toes. Her eyes widened and her cheeks suffused with that wonderful pink blush of hers.

Suddenly he wasn't in the least bit hungry. Not for food, anyway. He wanted to find out just exactly what was going on here. Why his physical response to this woman, this veterinarian from this little tiny town, was lighting him up like a Christmas tree.

"May I be excused? I have better things to do than watch you two flirt."

Alex looked at Chloe. Then at her mother.

"We are not flirting," Dani said quite firmly.

"No? I saw him touch you. I watched you blush. Then you looked down and fluttered your eyelashes like this."

Chloe demonstrated, but Alex thought she went a little too far.

"According to the 'Discovery Channel,' that's combining phase one and two of the courtship ritual."

"No more TV for you, young lady," Dani said, her flush brighter than ever.

"Hey, that's an educational channel. You're the one always pushing me to use my TV hours wisely."

"Well, I was wrong. Don't watch anything. Paint. Read. Cure male-pattern baldness." Dani stood up. "You're excused, you little troublemaker. Go do your homework."

Chloe shot from her chair, and for a moment, she looked like a perfectly ordinary little kid running to her room. But Alex knew she was nothing of the kind. He realized then who she reminded him of. Ted. She was a female, very miniature version of his majordomo. Of course she didn't look like him, but damn if she didn't behave like him.

"You think she was right?" he said, now that he was alone with Dani.

"No," she said, her vehemence practically knocking him off his seat.

"Does the lady protest too much?"

Dani took her plate and Chloe's to the kitchen without responding. But when she came back, she looked him straight in the eye. "I do not protest too much. You're here for a couple of days, max. Then you're off to the big city and your important life, and your supermodel girlfriends. I think it's probably a wise idea to remember that while you're in my home. I don't think one less notch on your belt is going to destroy your overall average. So let's keep it light, shall we?"

"A notch on my belt?"

"How you keep score isn't relevant."

"What makes you think I keep score at all?"

He didn't care for the look she gave him. Impatience mixed with censure. No, he didn't like it one bit. He rose and walked to her. Close. She didn't back away, he'd give that to her. But that's all.

"Look, Dr. Jacobson. Despite your utter contempt for whatever lifestyle you imagine I have, I am not the one who stood on tiptoe, who wanted a kiss so badly I could have felt the pull from across the state line."

"I didn't—"

He silenced her with his hungry gaze. God, he wanted to kiss her. Kiss her long and hard. Taste that sweet mouth of hers and feel her breasts against his chest. He felt himself harden. He wanted her to feel that. To know what she did to him.

But he didn't do a thing, except let her know that he was completely aware that keeping it light was impossible.

She knew it, too. He could see it in her eyes, in the lift of her brows. Then she touched her lower lip with her tongue, and there were absolutely no doubts left.

"I thought you wanted to go see Pete," she said, her voice suddenly much lower. Much breathier, although nothing like Caroline's asthmatic wheeze.

"I do," he said, not missing the changes in his own voice.

"So let's go."

"Okay."

She didn't make a move. He didn't, either. He just kept staring at her. His gaze swept over every inch of her face, memorizing every millimeter. She had a small scar on her right temple. Barely noticeable. Maybe a quarter of an inch. His hand moved toward it and he brushed his thumb against the little imperfection that seemed, somehow, to make her even more beautiful. As he made contact, Dani's eyes closed. She leaned into his touch, and again the urge to kiss her washed over him powerfully. If she stayed this way one more second, he wouldn't be responsible for his actions.

But she opened her eyes and moved back just enough to break the connection between them.

"I fell off my bike when I was a girl," she said.

He nodded. "I would have liked to have known you, then."

"You would?"

"Yes. I bet you were a lot like Chloe."

She shook her head slowly, still staring at him as hard as he was staring at her. "I was never that smart."

"No? Why don't I believe that?"

"It's true."

"But you were just as headstrong, weren't you?"

She nodded.

"Still are, for that matter."

"Worse."

He smiled and was rewarded by her lips turning up at the corners. He could see a hint of her even white teeth, and a small dimple very close to her mouth. Her very seductive mouth.

"Pete," she said.

He nodded absently. "Headstrong and beautiful."

Her eyes widened just a hair. "I'm not."

"Not what?"

"Beautiful."

"You're kidding, right? Of course you are." The second he'd spoken the words, something shifted. She pulled back. It wasn't a physical move, but an emotional snap. The invisible tie between them was severed in an instant, and although she was still close enough to kiss, the welcome mat had been snatched away.

She turned abruptly and walked to the table. She gathered plates and silverware, all business now.

"Dani?"

"We should go. Let me just put these up. I need to call Mimi to come watch Chloe for a few minutes."

"Let me help," he said, moving to the table. He wouldn't press her. But he thought her reaction to his compliment was very telling. And oddly endearing. He was used to women who were so confident about their beauty it actually became a tactical weapon. In his world, beauty was a commodity, used often and well. The game was silent, but the stakes were quite real.

He remembered seeing Dani for the first time, and he wondered how he'd ever considered her just "okay." Probably just because she didn't look like every female he knew—who spent more money on makeup than some third world countries spent on food. Or that she didn't look like the models she was so convinced he dated.

So okay, he had dated a few, but never anyone he'd really liked. He didn't care for women that thin. He much preferred Dani's soft curves. Her womanly shape. She would feel so good in his arms.

She walked away from him, carrying the covered dishes. He took the liberty of eyeing her backside. It was certainly a nice one. Very touchable. Although he doubted his touch would be welcome.

Forcing himself to get that image out of his brain, he picked up the remaining dishes and glasses from the table. By the time he had them on the counter in the kitchen, Dani was on the phone with her sitter. The conversation was brief, and then Dani was next to him at the sink.

"She'll be over in a second. I'll just put these in the dishwasher and then I'll go tell Chloe."

"I can do it," he said.

"No, it's okay."

He touched her arm. Zap. Damn, it was getting ridiculous. Just an innocent touch, and he still felt the flow from her body as if it were a current. He quickly drew back. "I'd like to."

Dani chanced a glance at him. She wondered if he'd felt the jolt. One look at his face and she knew he had. Why? Why this man? How come he was the one to awaken such unwelcome responses?

"Okay," she said, figuring distance was the safest possible course. "I'll be back in a moment." She hurried to Chloe's room, anxious to get away from whatever the heck was happening between her and Alex.

Chloe proved to be a good distraction. Her daughter was sitting on her bed, reading. She glanced down at the title: *Animal Farm.* "Haven't you read that one before?"

Chloe shook her head. "You're thinking of *Brave New World.*"

"Right." She tapped Chloe's legs. "Skootch over."

Chloe moved, and Dani sat down next to her. "Mimi's coming over. I'm taking Mr. Bradley to the clinic to see his dog."

"She doesn't have to. I'm perfectly capable of taking care of myself."

"Don't even start with me. I'm too tired to play tonight."

"Mom?"

Dani was surprised at the abrupt change in Chloe's tone. She sounded quite like an eight-year-old. "Hmm?"

"You *were* flirting with him, you know."

"It might have appeared that way for a second, but no, hon. Nothing like that is going on."

Her daughter's gaze searched her face, and Dani knew that the lie wasn't going to work. It never did with Chloe.

"It's because he's so handsome, right? I mean, for an old guy."

Dani smiled. "Well, he is good-looking. I'll concede to that."

"So, like, are you going to kiss him?"

"Chloe! What kind of a question is that?"

"Well, that program I was watching. The guy said that kissing was next. I just wondered, that's all."

"Why can't you watch 'MTV' like every other eight-year-old?"

Chloe rolled her eyes. "Like I could stand that junk."

Dani reached over and grabbed her girl by the cheeks and brought her close for a smooch. "That's the only kissing I'm going to be doing."

"I don't know. Maybe you *ought* to kiss him."

"Why?"

"I don't know. I've just never seen you flirt before. Desmond Morris, the guy from the show, he says it's a natural biological function. He's studied this stuff. He says we're supposed to have all these urges to mate and everything. That it's what makes us part of the cycle of life."

Dani released her daughter's face and stood up. "Desmond Morris has never studied my love life. So you know, Chloe, just because a woman finds a man attractive, doesn't mean she wants him for a mate."

"Why not?"

"Because there are a lot more important things that go into the process than physical attraction."

"Like what?"

Dani sighed. She'd hoped to avoid this sort of conversation—at least for a few years. It wasn't always easy having a daughter who was eight going on thirty. "Personality, mostly. Common interest and goals. Values. Honesty. Kindness. And many more."

Chloe nodded slowly. "He likes Monet."

Dani smiled. "That's not enough, kiddo. Now if I'm not back by eight-thirty, I don't want you to give Mimi any trouble about going to bed. All right?"

Chloe nodded again. Dani leaned down and kissed her once more, then walked toward the door.

"Mom?"

She stopped. "Yes?"

"I think he's nice."

"He is nice. But he's just going to be here a day or so."

"Okay."

"I'll try to get back to tuck you in."

Dani closed the door behind her. She didn't rush right to the kitchen, though. Her thoughts were on Desmond Morris and biology. She'd already determined that the thing that was happening to her was simple chemistry. Pheromones at work. What she didn't know was just how strong this chemistry business was. It wouldn't do to underestimate this kind of thing. She'd done that once, and she didn't want to be a fool again.

The best course of action was to stay as far away from Alex as she could. Scent distance away.

She heard a loud crash and the splintering of broken glass. Now she hurried.

Alex was standing in the middle of the kitchen, staring at the broken water glass on the floor. When he saw her, he looked up. "Oops."

She smiled. He sounded so young, so embarrassed. It was tempting to tease him, but she held back. "It's okay. No harm done."

"I'll be happy to replace it."

"I don't think that's going to be possible."

"Is it a family heirloom or something?"

"No. But I don't think Kmart is giving these away anymore."

He looked at her quizzically. Damn, he probably didn't even know what Kmart was. "It's a chain of discount stores. Sometimes they give premiums, like glasses, or free boxes of detergents."

His mouth formed a thin line, and his face turned just the slightest shade of pink. "I've heard of Kmart."

"But you've never been to one, right?"

"Snob," he said.

"Me?"

He nodded. "Yeah, you. Now where's the dustpan?"

She walked to the utility closet and got out the

broom. "You know, maybe it wouldn't do you any harm to stop by our local Kmart tomorrow. It just might broaden your horizons."

She went to sweep up the glass, but he took the broom and dustpan from her hand. When he bent, she caught a glimpse of his back, the muscles bunching beneath his white shirt. Wow.

"I'm not so terrible," he said as he swept. "It's not like I don't know any poor people."

"Some of your best friends are poor, right?"

He stood, and she pointed him to the trash. Once he'd dumped the mess, he turned to her again. "I like to think that I value people for who they are, not their gross income."

She took in a deep breath. "Okay, uncle. I'm not being fair, am I?"

He shook his head. "Not all rich folks are slime. Some of us are even pretty decent."

"I know. I'm sorry."

"Okay then."

She could tell he wasn't really upset, although she was. It wasn't like her to stereotype people. But with Alex it was difficult. He just exemplified so much of what she'd learned to distrust and dislike. But she didn't dislike him, did she? He was much nicer than she'd ever anticipated. Which didn't mean she was going to let down her guard. Randy had been nice at first, too.

She remembered the scent distance edict, and moved toward the open dishwasher. Alex had loaded the dishes in somewhat proper order, but he'd also put them in just as they'd come off the tables. He hadn't rinsed them at all. There were even two napkins in the lower shelf. "Do many dishes at your place, Alex?"

"Why? Did I do something wrong?"

"Well, yes and no. You got everything in the right place, but you left the food on them."

"What do you mean?"

"You have to rinse the dishes, first," she said, turning on the water in the sink.

"That doesn't seem right. It's a dishwasher. Why should you have to wash the dishes before you put them in?"

"I don't know why. I just know that this way, they won't end up clean."

"Seems a waste of time."

"So much of life is."

"Is that another shot at me?"

She turned to him as she started to unload the plates. "No. Just commentary. For someone like me, there's a lot of little things to do. Make beds. Do laundry. Shop for food. Cook dinner. With the clinic, and with Chloe, it doesn't leave much time for the rest of life."

"I could help. While I'm here, I mean."

She laughed. "I appreciate the offer, but I don't think you'd make a very good maid."

"Hey, I'm a quick study. And I'm not helpless. As long as I'm here, I see no reason not to pitch in. I know this isn't a hotel. I'd like to do my share.''

Her first instinct was to say no. She couldn't for the life of her imagine Alex Bradley doing a load of laundry. But she hesitated. Maybe the best thing for the Sexiest Man in the World to do was exactly that. He wanted real life? She'd give him real life.

She turned to him and stuck out a wet hand. "Okay. I accept your offer."

He grasped her palm, and the jolt came back. Uh-oh. It wasn't enough to keep scent distance apart. She must remember not to touch.

"Just tell me what to do."

The doorbell rang then. "Let Mimi in for starters," she said.

Alex nodded, but he didn't drop her hand just yet. He held it gently. Carefully. Then she felt his thumb move over her skin. It was a delicate move, almost imperceptible. Yet she felt herself go all goose bumps.

She pulled away. Funny, though. It didn't help much. She could still feel his touch even as he walked out of the room.

Chapter Five

Alex closed the door behind Dani, and walked with her down the path to the sidewalk. The night air felt great. Just chilly enough for the light jackets they both wore. Dani walked a little ahead of him, and he took a moment to appreciate the fact that her black jacket came only to her waist, leaving her very inviting denim-clad derrière uncovered. While he wasn't ordinarily a butt man, he realized she might be able to swing the vote.

Instead of heading to her car, she led him down the sidewalk. He joined her quickly and soon they were striding next to each other on the well-lit street. His hands were in his pockets, as were hers. They were just far enough apart so that a random brush of the shoulder was unlikely.

He thought about moving closer to her, but he didn't. His reactions to this virtual stranger were strong. Strong enough to make him concerned. He didn't like the feeling that he wasn't completely in control of his emotions. One thing Alex had learned from his father: It's a fool who lets his gonads do his thinking for him.

But damn, his gonads felt awfully determined this time. Lust was something he respected, and when appropriate, he liked to respond. With Dani, it wasn't appropriate. End of story. Best to concentrate on his surroundings, and get his mind away from thoughts of derrières and gonads.

"So you've always lived here, have you?" he said, hoping his impromptu opening line didn't sound as lame to her as it did to him.

"Yes."

They continued walking. Silently. The street itself held little out of the ordinary. Just a quiet block of family homes. Some folks had left the drapes open so he could see tiny snippets of domestic life as they walked by. A family of five at dinner. "Wheel of Fortune" playing on a couple of TVs. Some kid practicing the piano. It was ordinary, all right, and completely unfamiliar to him. He'd never spent any time in suburbia. The homes he visited usually had long driveways, butlers or maids to open the doors. Foyers big enough to fit two cars comfortably. He was a stranger here. As out of place as a bug on a cream puff. Yet he found himself interested in this world of Dani's.

"Have any desire to live anywhere else?" he said. This time, the question wasn't just intended to break the silence. He wanted to know what it was about this town that kept her here. That made her work so hard to succeed in it.

"Not really," she said. "This is my home. It's got its problems, but basically it's a good place to live. A good place for Chloe."

"They have special programs for her?"

"Yes, Mr. Bradley. Even here in Mayberry we've heard of accelerated programs for exceptional children."

"I got that, you know. Mayberry. Andy Griffith. Opie. Aunt Bea."

She slowed and looked up at him. The angle was just perfect, too. Her face was lit by a street lamp, the color of a soft tan. Her skin seemed to glow. Her teeth, when she smiled, were as white as new snow.

"Very good. I'm surprised they let you watch what the common folks watched."

"Tell me something, Dani. Did a gang of rich people come and beat you up when you were a kid? Steal your dog? Take away the homestead?"

She coughed, and looked away. She started walking again, more quickly this time.

"Uh-uh," he said, reaching out and grabbing her by the arm. She stopped, but she didn't turn to him.

"Come on, Doc. Tell me why you hate my kind so much. I'm a big boy. I can take it."

"I don't hate your kind," she said, but she didn't try to break free of his hold.

"So it's me personally? Right? I said something wrong? I wore the wrong shoes?"

She didn't move for a long while. He wasn't sure what she was looking at, only that she wasn't looking at him. He wanted to prod her into her explanation, but he forced himself to wait. He didn't want a smart-ass answer. He wanted the truth.

Finally she did look at him again. He let her arm go, knowing she wasn't going to run away.

"I'm sorry. I've really been out of line. It's not you. It has nothing to do with you."

"Who then?"

"Someone I used to like very much."

"He was rich, I assume?"

She smiled in a way that made him clench his teeth. "No, but he wanted to be. Very, very badly."

He waited a moment to see if she was going to say more, and when she didn't, he began to walk again. He didn't even look back to see if she followed, but in a few steps he felt her next to him.

It wasn't easy to keep his questions to himself, but he wasn't going to press. He wasn't even sure why he wanted to. But for some reason, he was upset by her very small revelation, and found himself wanting to fix it.

"I'll bet it's made your life pretty easy," she said quietly, as they crossed the street that bordered the commercial section of town. There were other people walking now, strolling, as they were. Funny to see no cars moving, and folks out and about. It happened in Los Angeles, of course. People still did use their legs on occasion, but the feel was different here. The pace was what he wasn't used to. The folks he saw might be headed somewhere specific, but then again, they might not.

"Some things were easier, I guess," he said. "But I think it's all relative. There were expectations, demands. My choices were pretty limited."

"Limited? I would think the world would be at your feet."

He shook his head. "Only in the sense that I could get from here to there. No, I knew who and what I was supposed to be from the moment I was born. Everything was geared in that direction. My education, my friends, my social life."

"What, you're going to tell me that you really wanted to be a circus clown or something?"

He laughed. "No. It didn't work that way. I just did what I was supposed to, and made myself want it."

They passed a brightly lit ice-cream parlor where an older couple sat at a small table sipping sodas. Alex saw that they were holding hands under the table. It was almost too much. Too Stepford. But then he saw, right in back of the old couple, a little kid pull a wad of gum from underneath a table and stick it in his sister's hair. As they reached the post office next door, he heard the wail of the girl, who'd clearly discovered the bit of mischief.

"Do you still want it?" Dani asked.

"Yes," he said, quickly. "Well, a lot of it. Things have changed in the last couple of years, though."

"Like what?"

He saw her office just down the block. He was anxious to see Pete. The old pooch usually slept in his bedroom, and he was probably wondering what the heck was going on. "I've met the expectations," he said. "And I guess I'm just wondering what's next."

"What new mountain to climb?"

"Something like that. Maybe wondering if I want to climb at all. That's why I'm out here. I've never driven cross-country before. Never felt I had the time. I think that's the thing money really does for you, if you let it."

"What?"

"Give you some time."

They were at the clinic, and Dani brought out her key to open the door. Once they were inside the dark office, he heard the sounds of the pets in the back. A little yappy dog set the pace, and then a couple of other, bigger dogs joined in. He didn't hear Pete, though.

She turned on the light and led him into the inner sanctum. Her unhurried pace from just a moment ago was gone, and in its place was purpose. She moved quickly and easily, in command of her space. He'd been right to leave Pete in her care.

They got to the back room, and she switched on

the light. Pete was on his feet in the big cage. Alex could already see that the old guy was a little better. Pete's whole body wagged, not quite as enthusiastically as normal, but still pretty good. Alex smiled as he heard the familiar greeting whine, and he went over and put his hand through the wide cage and grabbed the old boy.

DANI WATCHED ALEX greet his pet. He crouched down, and let Pete lick his face. Pete looked better. The liquids and the medication were working, although he wasn't ready to leave yet. She'd still have to keep her eyes on him for a couple of days. A dog his age was liable to take a sudden turn.

But for now, Pete looked comfortable. Before they left, she would give him a brief exam and listen to his lungs. Now, though, she would leave the man and his pet alone for their moment, and take a look at her other patients.

She went first to the bulldog with the broken leg. As she comforted the big guy she heard Pete's cage door open. Glancing back, she watched as Alex crawled inside. He sat Indian-style on the big pillow, and Pete curled up in his lap like a pup.

She felt a lump rise in her throat and turned away. What a ridiculous response. But then, her responses to Alex Bradley had all been pretty ridiculous.

She'd known him for only a few hours. Yet he'd made her think of things she had no business thinking. Brought up memories best left undisturbed. She had treated him unfairly, and it rankled that she could be so petty. Especially when he'd been so open with his own story.

The bulldog was doing well, and after a few minutes of petting him, listening to the soft, unintelligible conversation Alex was having with Pete, she turned to a young tabby kitten who'd been caught in some barbed wire. The little one mewled at her pitifully, but Dani saw that she'd eaten her food and had plenty of water. Her wounds were on the mend. The cat really just needed attention. All of the creatures she cared for did. No matter what medicines and surgical techniques she used to heal the wounded pets, the one thing she believed in most was a loving hand. A gentle touch.

She lifted the cat to her chest, and turned to watch Alex. He had quieted, and now she saw why. He was still petting Pete, but his gaze was on her. He looked at her the way she knew she looked at her charges. With concern, with patience, with care. Why? She'd been nothing but snarly with him. Yet his look was genuine.

He really did care. About her. A stranger, not someone in her huge ever-expanding family, or the town that had helped raise her. This was a sophisticated, intelligent man. Someone who owed her nothing, needed nothing back.

"He's better," Alex said.

"I can see that. I'd like to check him out before we go."

"You want me to come out?"

She shook her head. "I have a few more patients to tend to first."

He smiled. "I don't think that one's going to let you."

She looked down at the kitten. Her small gray head was burrowed against her chin, and the little claws were kneading her chest in a rhythmic motion that all children, no matter what species, seemed to know. Her purr was loud for such a teeny thing. "You're right."

"Is that one a stray?"

"No. She's got a home. A good one. She's just used to a lot of attention."

"Yeah, that's how it is, I guess. You get spoiled." He turned to the third cage down from Pete's. Inside was a white mutt, the only dog who hadn't moved or barked since they'd arrived. "What's his story?"

"The other side of the coin," Dani said. "He's not had it very easy, from what I could see. He'd been beaten up pretty badly. Lost a lot of blood."

"A stray?"

"Worse. We took him from his owner. The jerk had mistreated him for years. The poor thing doesn't know what a loving touch is."

She looked at the dog, alone, scared, wounded.

When Alex spoke, it took her a minute to register his words.

"Do you?"

"What do you mean?" she asked, although she knew.

"I keep thinking you want to be like that kitten, but you're afraid, like that white dog."

"Bold assessment for a man I've known only a few hours."

"I haven't known the critters here for five minutes, but it's not hard to tell who's who and what's what."

She put the kitten back in the small cage, cringing at the distressed sounds the little one made. Walking slowly, carefully, she approached the wounded dog. As she neared he stood up on shaky legs, his hackles rose and he bared his teeth. She waited patiently, letting the dog get her scent. She'd avoided a muzzle this morning, and she wanted to again now. While she gave the dog time to calm down, she thought about Alex's comment. Was it true?

"Hey, Dani?"

She nodded.

"Forget it. I'm sorry. I don't know you well enough to be spouting off like that."

"No, you don't. But it's okay. Who knows. Maybe there's even some truth to it."

"Aw, what do I know?"

She turned to meet his gaze. "Too much, I think."

He looked at her for a long while. "I know one other thing."

"What's that?"

"It would be a damn shame."

"What?"

"For you to stay in that cage."

DANI LOCKED THE DOOR behind them. She'd finished checking all the animals, including Pete, who was indeed doing a lot better, and now she wanted to get home. Things had certainly shifted on this innocent little trip. Suddenly Alex wasn't just some rich stranger she felt vaguely annoyed about. And vaguely turned on by. Now he was a person, flesh and blood and three dimensional, which was a much more serious problem.

Who would have thought this man would have been so insightful? Could have seen her so clearly? Not that he was a hundred percent accurate about her, but there was some truth to his words. He'd given her something to think about. But she wasn't going to do that now. Not with him. He'd leave in a day or so, and then she'd take some time and think it over.

She pocketed her key and they headed home. The street was quieter now. A few places were still open. The ice-cream parlor, the drugstore. But by nine, the town would be bedded down for the night.

As they neared the ice-cream shop, she felt Alex's hand touch her gently on the small of the back. His hand only made contact with her jacket, and still it was enough to shake her out of her reverie. This was something entirely new. Even Randy's touch hadn't made her so physically aware. But Alex... All he had to do was brush her gently, and sparks flew.

"How about some ice cream?" he asked.

She debated for a moment. But only a moment. "Sure, I'd like that."

"Great." He walked a little quicker, and his tentative touch on her back grew stronger. She felt the heat through her jacket, and wondered if he noticed it.

At the parlor, Alex took his hand away, and opened the door for her. She walked in, suddenly very thirsty for something very cold.

Janet Colby, a local high school senior, was behind the counter. Dani almost laughed at the girl's reaction to Alex. Her face, normally very pale, got quite red. Her hand went immediately to her hair, and the little white paper hat she wore. Her gaze swung wildly, but always came back to Alex.

Dani could relate. He did have a way of flustering a person.

"Dr. Jacobson," the girl said, finally. "Um..."

"Hi, Janet. This is Mr. Bradley. We'd like to get some ice cream."

"Uh-huh," Janet said, nodding, staring now.

"Nice to meet you, Janet," Alex said.

Dani was struck by the gentleness of his tone. The interest behind it. She doubted very much that he wanted to become friends with the girl behind the counter, but he made it sound as if it was a real possibility.

"Can you excuse me for a second?" Janet said.

Before Dani could answer, the girl was gone, ducked into the back room.

"I'll bet that happens a lot."

Alex smiled. "More than I'd like."

"It's kinda sweet."

"No, it's kind of embarrassing. I am not cut out for this sort of thing."

"On the contrary," she said as she examined the flavors in the freezer case, "you are remarkably adept at it."

"What are you talking about?"

"Damn, they don't have mint chocolate chip."

"Don't change the subject."

"I meant," she said, "that you handle yourself very well. A lot of people in your situation wouldn't."

"What, because I say hello to people?"

"Yes. That's exactly right."

"That's nothing."

She turned from the ice cream to face him. "No, it's not nothing. I've seen people like you behave quite badly to people like her. Just because they can."

"Well, then, some people you might think are like me, aren't like me at all."

Just then, before she could think how to respond to this latest little jolt to her ego, the door to the ice-cream parlor opened. A group of girls, seven of them, walked in. They all looked flushed, as if they'd been running. They probably had. Dani groaned. It was going to be another replay of this afternoon at the coffee shop. Janet hadn't gone to compose herself in the back room; she'd gone to set the jungle drums in motion.

"I think you're in for some company," she whispered.

"Uh-oh."

"Yeah. Wanna make a break for it?"

He shook his head, then looked fixedly at the Chocolate Chocolate Chip. "Not yet."

"It's up to you."

The bell above the door jingled again, and Dani watched another three high school kids come in. The place wasn't all that big, and now there were a lot of people here. Yet it was awfully quiet. No one needed to speak. They just needed to stare. At the Sexiest Man in the World.

Suddenly Dani felt sorry for Alex. She'd seen he was a person, not the picture on the magazine cover. This couldn't be easy for him.

Janet came out from the back, and flushed again as she saw her friends lining the back wall. She tried to smile, but it wasn't very convincing.

Dani ordered quickly, her tone a little accusatory. But when Alex asked for his double scoop of chocolate chip and jamoca, his voice held no bitterness.

Janet worked with shaky hands, and the cones were less than masterpieces. Dani was getting jumpy. More kids entered the parlor, but no one said one word. It was eerie and uncomfortable, and all she wanted to do was get out and apologize profusely to her guest. What were these kids thinking?

Alex took his cone, and grabbed a few napkins. "How much is it?" he asked.

"Four-twenty," Janet said, her voice cracking a little at the end.

He gave her a five, and while they waited for the change, someone coughed. Not a big cough, but a "I'm going to say something" cough.

"Mr. Bradley?"

The voice came from a girl Dani didn't know. She was the smallest one there. Cute, dark haired, wearing an "X-Files" T-shirt and very tight jeans.

Alex turned to face her. "Yes?"

"Could I have your autograph, you think?"

He nodded, smiling. "Sure. You have some paper?"

The girl shook her head. "Not on paper." She held out her arm as she walked closer. "On here."

Dani nearly dropped her ice cream.

Alex merely nodded. "Got a pen?"

The girl handed him a permanent marker. Blue. Dani watched in amazement as Alex put his ice cream in the holder on the counter, calmly un-capped the pen, took the teenager's arm and wrote his name boldly.

He smiled at the girl, and she giggled. Then an-other girl, this one taller and blond, came to take her place. She held out her arm. "Me, too?"

Alex nodded. Smiled. Signed.

Dani licked her cone as she watched every one of the young women stand and wait their turn. He was patient, pleasant and even made some conver-sation with the starstruck girls.

She was truly amazed. Why anyone would want an autograph like this was beyond her, but she'd been a kid once, and remembered she'd done some crazy things. But more amazing was watching Alex. He simply couldn't have surprised her more.

Finally the last girl stood in front of him. He reached for her arm, but she shook her head. Instead she pulled up her little crop-top T-shirt, baring a very slender, very tanned midriff.

Alex immediately turned to look at Dani, smiled and winked. It was a conspiratorial smile, meant just for her. A shared moment that sent a little shiver up her spine. It wasn't because he was fa-mous. It was because he was Alex.

Chapter Six

"So, it's not the first time you've written on some-one's tummy?"

Alex shook his head. As he and Dani crossed the last street toward home he slowed down a bit. He didn't want this walk to end. The hell with the walk, he didn't want Dani's laughter to end. "No, this was my second tummy."

"What other body parts have you written on?"

"Well," he said, licking the ice-cream cone that had replaced the melted one. "I wrote the secret lyrics to 'Louie, Louie' on my hand in high school."

"Secret lyrics?"

"Yeah, you know. The ones after 'We gotta go now.'"

"I thought those were, 'Yeah, yeah, yeah, yeah, yeah.'"

He shrugged. "I guess they weren't so secret."

She laughed again. God, that sound! It made his chest swell, not to mention another key appendage.

She was in the light of the street lamp now so he could really see her smile. Damn, but she was appealing. It would be nice to see her face, with that smile, last thing before he went to sleep. Or the first thing when he woke up. If only...

If only, what? If she were living in New York instead of New Mexico? If he was the kind of man who could live in a place like Carlson's Gap?

"Doesn't it make you feel awkward, though? All the attention, I mean."

He shook his head. "It's temporary. I'm the flavor of the month, that's all. Very soon, I'll be that guy that was in the magazine, and right after that I'll be someone who might have been someone, once. What's the harm in playing it out?"

"The lack of privacy, for one."

"I have the kind of privacy that matters."

"Oh?"

"They might know the face, but they don't know the man."

"Pity for them."

He stopped. "That's quite a compliment, coming from you. I'm going to have to buy you a lot more ice cream."

"Ice cream had nothing to do with it."

"Then what?"

She started walking again and he fell in beside her. They were much closer than they had been on the way to the clinic. And nobody's hands were in pockets. As a matter of fact, her hand was enticingly close to his. Close enough to hold, which is just what he did.

She looked first at their joined hands, then up at him. He wondered if she was going to pull away, but she didn't, even though she frowned. He'd have to watch his step.

"Okay, so I jumped to some wrong conclusions before," she said. "I'm sorry. You're not just some pretty rich guy—" She stopped speaking, and when he looked at her, she was studying the ground.

He frowned. "Go ahead. Finish the sentence. I can take it."

She sighed as she looked up at him. "Some pretty rich guy with an ego the size of Detroit."

"You shouldn't be so sure about that. I've got an ego all right."

"An ego is permissible. An ego that feeds on making other people feel small, isn't."

"I see. And as far as the pretty and rich part?"

"Also permissible. Although it is disconcerting to realize just how much prettier you are than me."

"Are you kidding?"

"Come on. It's true. You know you're gorgeous."

He tugged her to a stop, tossed his cone into a trash barrel in the driveway and turned her so he could look right at her. "Because we're such good friends, and because I've known you such a long time, I'm going to be very bold and tell you something, Dr. Jacobson."

"I don't think I want to hear it."

"Too bad. You're going to hear it anyway."

She sighed again. "You don't have to tell me I'm pretty. I wasn't fishing."

"I'm not going to tell you that."

"Gee, thanks."

"You're not pretty. Well, not just pretty. You're beautiful. And sexy. And intelligent. And desirable. But that's not the problem."

She didn't respond immediately. He watched her gaze sweep over his face, study his eyes. Her mouth opened slightly, as if she needed a little more breath. He was sure, if it had been daylight, he'd have seen color tint her cheeks. "What is?" she whispered.

"You don't know that you're beautiful. Sexy. Intelligent. And oh, so desirable," he whispered right back. Then he leaned down, slowly, and finally took the kiss that had been promised all those hours before.

The first touch of her lips was something he'd remember for the rest of his life. And never be able to describe. "Softness" wasn't adequate. "Sweet" didn't say it at all. The only thing close was heaven. His groin told him to crush her incredible lips with his, but he held back, wanting the torment to last. He tasted first, sipped. Licked her bottom lip. Teased her with the pressure, first soft, then harder, then soft again.

It was her moan that changed his mind. The dark,

throaty sound made him move closer, wrap his arms around her back. Bring her tight against his body so they touched from lips to thighs. He felt the tip of her tongue on his and then there was no more teasing. He let go, letting his body lead him. His tongue met hers and his thoughts turned primitive with raw hunger.

He wanted this woman in every way. He just couldn't get enough. His hands wanted to touch her back and her thighs and her knees, all at once. He wanted to taste her sweet breasts, but it was inconceivable to stop this kiss.

Her hands made it all worse. He felt her explorations, felt the urgency and the heat. She wanted him as he wanted her, but they were standing in the middle of the street with open windows all around them or he would have pulled her to the ground right there.

She broke the kiss and leaned her head on his shoulder for a second, breathing deeply. He closed his eyes, forcing himself to get it together. It wasn't easy. He was hard as a rock, straining against his pants, and every time she moved it was agony.

"Holy cow," she whispered.

"You can say that again," he said.

"Holy cow."

He smiled. "So, uh, isn't your house just down the block? Shouldn't we be heading there? Very, very quickly?"

Dani moved back, stepping out of his embrace. "I don't think so."

"Why?" he asked, amazed at how quickly his body reacted to the hesitant, apologetic tone in Dani's voice. His erection wasn't an urgent problem anymore, although one look from her and it would be a national emergency in a heartbeat.

"We shouldn't have done that," she said.

"Why not? It was pretty spectacular."

She shook her head. He kept staring at her mouth, the taste of her so present it made him ache.

"It was still foolish," she said. "It can't go anywhere."

"Why not, Dani? What would be the harm?"

"You're leaving."

"Not right now."

"Soon."

"Then let me leave you with a memory. A damn good memory."

"I've got enough of those, thanks."

"Not the right kind," he said. He reached over and touched her cheek with the back of his hand. Her eyes closed and she leaned into the caress. Her skin was magically soft and fragile. His want of her so powerful he was nearly knocked senseless.

Dani knew if she didn't do something soon, he would kiss her again. And if he kissed her again she would kiss him back. If she did that, she wouldn't be able to stop. She'd take him to her bed, and she'd make love with him and it would be wonderful and then what? She'd have memories all right. Memories that would torment her each long night she slept alone.

"I can't," she said.

"Why not?" he asked as he dropped his hand to his side. His gaze never left her, though, and the question there, the confusion, made her look away.

"I take these things pretty seriously," she said.

"You don't think I'm serious?"

"Yes. But not in the way I mean. You want to have sex. Which is fine. But I only want to make love."

He studied her for a long moment. She let him, wanting him to see that she wasn't condemning him for his desires. Wanting him to see her own regret.

"Dani?"

"Yes?"

"The only thing I'd ever want to do with you is make love."

He looked so earnest. If she hadn't known better, if she hadn't already learned this lesson the hard way, she would have believed him. "I'm not the kind of woman you're used to," she said. "I can't love someone for one night, and forget about it the next day."

"I know that."

"Then you know why I can't..." She couldn't finish the sentence. Not with him looking at her that way. So hurt. So hungry.

He leaned forward quickly and brushed her lips

with his. It was a quick kiss, almost not a kiss at all, yet she felt that spark between them. The pull to go into his arms was like a force of nature.

"Hey," he said. "It's all right." He took her hand in his and started walking again, heading toward her house at a leisurely pace. "But for the record, I'm not the playboy of the Western world. I do know the difference between having sex and making love."

"I'm sure you do."

"Uh-uh. There's that cynical tone again. Don't believe everything you read in the papers, Dani."

"You're telling me you've never had sex for sex's sake?"

"No."

"That you've never had a one-night stand?"

"No."

"Then what?"

He pulled her to a stop. They were just a few feet from her house. As she turned to look at him, she saw that her neighbor's window was open. She could hear the soft strains of classical music. Then she looked into Alex's eyes, and the rest of the world disappeared.

"What I'm telling you is that I know the difference," he said. "I know what it is to make love. To want to be close with your heart as well as your body. I know what it's like to have a lover in my arms. To care more about her than I care about breathing. You're not the only one with memories, kiddo.''

"Who was she?''

"Someone a lot like you. Feisty. Beautiful. Soft.''

"What happened?''

He smiled with such melancholy that it made her sorry she'd asked. "I sent her away.''

"Why?''

His eyes closed. The creases in his forehead deepened with a long remembered pain. "Because she didn't fit in to the plan,'' he said. "Loving her broke all the rules.''

"Rules?''

He opened his eyes, and looked at her once more. "Honey, you have no idea.''

"So tell me.''

"Maybe sometime. Now, I need to get you home. I think Chloe might be upset that I've kept you out so late.''

"If Chloe is up, she's not the one who's going to be upset.''

He smiled. "Come on, Doc. Let's call it a night.''

Dani let him lead her to the door. She wondered what he'd meant when he talked about the rules. What kind of rules could a man like him have to live by? The world was his oyster. She couldn't imagine him bending to anyone's standards but his own.

She entered the house, and the first thing she noticed was that too many lights were on. If all was well, the hall would be the only space lit, with the possible exception of the living room, if Mimi had decided to read instead of watch TV.

Dani looked quickly at Alex, then hurried toward Chloe's room. She never got there. Instead she stopped dead in her tracks at the entrance to the dining room. Mimi stood by the table. She was staring hard at a very large, very green iguana, who was looking right back at her from the vantage point of the center of the dining room table. The iguana had a leash, and Terry Redmond, a single mother of two who lived on the other side of town, was holding on to the other end. Dani happened to know the iguana. Better, in fact, than she knew Terry. The iguana's name was Filbert and he belonged to Terry's fifteen-year-old son.

But that wasn't all. Sitting next to Terry was Maureen Westbury. Maureen was also single. She ran the aerobics studio on Fourth Street, and normally dressed in either leotard and tights or jeans and a T-shirt. Tonight, she wore a black dress so tight there wasn't enough room for a breath of air between the dress and the woman. Maureen had a small fishbowl on her lap. With a single goldfish swimming idly in a circle.

To top off the spectacle, Keelyn Porter, a woman Dani had known all through grammar school and high school, was also sitting at the table. Keelyn, who Dani knew reasonably well, didn't own a pet. She didn't care for pets, and had told Dani that many times. Yet she had a cat on her lap. A live cat who didn't seem very pleased to be on her lap.

"They decided to wait," Mimi said, her voice sounding strained and anxious.

"I see," Dani said. She looked at the three women, ready to tell them that she had a clinic for a reason, but they weren't paying attention to her. Every eye was focused on Alex.

As she watched, three pairs of lips smiled. Three hands shot up to adjust three hairstyles. Three pairs of cheeks got pink and rosy.

Alex cleared his throat.

Then Filbert decided he was bored.

Iguanas can move pretty fast when they want to. So can cats.

Filbert darted across the table, heading right for Keelyn, jerking the leash out of Terry's hand. Mimi screamed first, which caused the cat to leap off Keelyn's lap and run straight toward Dani. Dani tried to head him off, and he veered left, then doubled back as Keelyn screeched. The cat went between Maureen's legs, causing her to jump to her feet and drop the fishbowl on the floor. The crash was loud enough to scare the hell out of Filbert who used Keelyn's back as a path to the ground.

Mimi continued screaming, as did Keelyn and Maureen. The cat found the drapes and scaled them, only to find that there was no immediate escape.

The fish flopped on the floor, and just as Dani was going to attempt that rescue, Alex moved. He scooped up the goldfish and headed for the kitchen. Dani only got a brief glance at him, but she could see his body shake. Wondering why he was so afraid of goldfish, she darted around the table trying to locate the ever popular Filbert.

Mimi ran from the room, straight down the hall and out the front door. Dani found Filbert eyeing the cat who was still hanging by his claws from the drapes. Just then Chloe wandered in, a look of abject fear on her face.

Dani abandoned the iguana to take care of Chloe. But Chloe was too busy staring at Keelyn, who continued to screech like a badly tuned violin.

"Keelyn!" Dani shouted. "It's all right. The fish will be fine."

Keelyn stopped her caterwauling and stared at her. "Who cares about the fish. The damn lizard went to the bathroom on my back!"

Dani froze. She looked at Chloe, who looked so confused she just might start crying. Then she heard the laughter come rolling in from the kitchen, and she lost it herself.

She laughed so hard she started crying, and when she tried to get the cat from the drapes, she couldn't do it. The cat hissed, Dani snorted in a most unladylike fashion, and then she turned to see Alex standing in the doorway, tears running down his contorted face, trying to hold a water glass with a goldfish in it.

She couldn't stand it. The laughter hurt her stomach and her sides, and she just kind of sat down on the floor. She definitely couldn't look at Alex. Chloe came up to her, still confused and scared, and Dani held out her arms.

Chloe blinked, then sat down, too. At least the screaming had stopped, although now Keelyn was trying to get the cat down by stomping her feet and shouting, "Come! Heel!"

Maureen walked over to Alex, her back quite straight and stiff, and snatched the water glass from him. She sniffed once, turned and walked out of the dining room to the door and out.

Terry was trying to corner Filbert. The cat growled from the drapes. Keelyn looked at Dani as if this was all somehow her fault.

Dani took a couple of deep breaths and wiped her eyes. "Whose cat is it, Keelyn?"

"My nephew's."

"Is something wrong with it?"

"How the hell would I know?"

"Why did you bring it here?"

Keelyn stopped. She turned to look at Alex who was just starting to breathe normally again. He, too, wiped his eyes with the back of his hand. "Think about it, Dani."

"Yeah," she said, climbing to her feet. "I suppose it's the same thing with you, Terry, right?"

"Just help me get this monster back in my car, okay?" Terry said in a stage whisper that Alex was sure to hear. "I don't want to talk about it."

"That's okay with me." She held out her hand to Chloe, who took it and stood. "You, young lady, need to go back to bed."

"I'm too awake now."

"I think you ladies were looking for this?"

Dani turned. Alex had Filbert in his hands, which were stuck out quite far in front of him. The iguana didn't seem to mind. He just blinked one eye, then the other.

Terry blushed and hurried to fetch Filbert. She managed to grab him without once making eye contact with Alex. Then she practically ran out of the house, her high heels clicking noisily on the tile.

Only one more to go. Keelyn. With her very damp dress and her embarrassed frown. Dani walked over to the woman and put her hand on her arm. Quietly, trying to preserve some dignity for the poor thing, she said, "Don't worry about the cat. You can tell your nephew to fetch him tomorrow at the clinic."

Keelyn nodded. She started to say something, then she stopped. Dani took that second to glance over at Alex. He was smiling broadly, watching her. His hair was mussed, his jacket off. He leaned against the doorjamb as if he'd been there a hundred nights. His look at her was deeply amused, and very intense. She thought of his kiss, and his invitation, and she wanted him all over again.

"How do you do that?" Keelyn whispered.

Dani had forgotten she was still there. "What?"

"Get these gorgeous men to lust after you like that?"

"What?"

"He looks so much like Randy it's scary. And man, does he ever have the hots for you."

Dani straightened immediately. Keelyn's words were like a cold slap in the face. "You're way off base."

Keelyn shook her head. "Nope. It's high school all over again. And you've got the captain of the football team in your living room. I just don't get it..." She gasped a little and stepped closer. "I didn't mean it the way it sounded. I mean, you're so cute and smart and all, of course any man would like you. It's just that—"

"The clinic opens at nine," she said. "Good night, Keelyn."

The woman backed up some more, clearly anxious to get out after her faux pas. "I mean it, Dani. You're just darling. Honest."

"Good night, Keelyn."

Dani watched her old high school acquaintance leave. Boy, some things never changed. How the girls in class used to wonder, aloud, in front of her, how she, plain little Dani Jacobson, could possibly have attracted Randy, of all people. It was a mystery gone unsolved until the day Randy had walked out of her life. That was a move everyone seemed to understand. Herself included.

Chapter Seven

Alex tried to remember the last time he'd laughed so hard he cried. He couldn't. He continued to smile, even as Dani left to put Chloe back to bed. The cat was still on the loose, but other than that, the house was quiet once more, and Alex debated going up to his room. Dani may not come out again, but he hoped she would. He wanted to talk to her. To see her laugh.

An odd feeling of déjà vu swept over him, and he remembered a girl he'd known as a child. Denise Gillard. She'd been his first best friend. They'd played in the woods behind his house every day all summer long. She'd been chubby, and pretty, and she'd laughed like no one he'd met since. Well, until Dani. It was infectious laughter, the kind that grew and grew until they'd had to simply lay down on the grass because their legs wouldn't hold them anymore.

Dani had laughed that way tonight. He'd seen her on the floor, unselfconscious, abandoned. He tried to picture her doing that in the dining room of his house. No, she wouldn't have. His place was too formal for sitting-on-the-floor kind of laughter. When had that happened? At what juncture of his life had he opted for formality over comfort? Polished over casual?

He hadn't been like that in college. His fraternity room had been a typical hodgepodge of beer bottles, empty pizza boxes and babe posters. Then he'd moved to the Green Hill apartment. His father had sent that decorator. Alex hadn't objected. Hell, he'd been thrilled. The apartment was a young man's dream. Good leather couches, framed artwork on the walls. Matching towels. He'd been comfortable there, pleased that he could have such a nice place right after graduation. The girls had loved coming over.

But even then, he'd given something up. Some little piece of himself. The babe posters had gone, the beer bottles relegated to the wet bar, and the maid had disposed of any pizza boxes before they had a chance to hit the floor. College may have been over, but his education had just begun. He was the prince regent, the next in line to inherit his father's millions, and that meant doing things the Bradley way.

Alex went to the fridge and studied the contents. He got out the carton of milk and found himself a glass. He poured, grabbed a package of Oreos, then went back out to sit at the dining-room table.

He remembered sitting at the table in his brand-new apartment all those years ago. His father had taken the seat across from him. Alexander, Senior, had told him then that while it was fine to have fun with all kinds of women, it was not fine to get serious about just anyone. He'd laid out the rules, clearly, definitively.

Alex's own mother had fit the criteria for a Bradley wife to a T. She'd been beautiful, extraordinarily so. A sterling hostess, and an attentive—if somewhat distant—mother. She never interfered in business, never seemed to mind that her husband had a constant stream of other women on the side. She shopped a great deal, did her charity work and made the circuit of parties from Beverly Hills to Monaco to Switzerland.

Felicity Bradley had died five years ago in a car accident. She'd been in Park City, Utah, on a skiing trip. When Alex had flown out to get her body, he'd discovered she'd had her own lover: a ski instructor a year younger than him.

It hadn't shocked him. On the contrary. He'd felt happy for her. At least she'd gotten some joy of her own.

Was he going to have to get his joy from affairs? Would a woman like Dani ever agree to being the other woman? He doubted it.

Funny thing. The rules had been a part of his life since before puberty. He'd accepted them, just as he'd accepted that he would go to Harvard, that he would take over the business. But now, sitting here dunking his cookie, waiting for a small town vet to leave her daughter's bedside, he was actually thinking that maybe, just maybe, the rules of the father didn't have to be the rules of the son.

"Where's *my* glass?"

He turned. Dani stood in the doorway, smiling at him. He had to smile back. "Pull up a seat," he said as he stood and headed for the kitchen. "One glass, coming right up."

He heard her sit down and he hurried. In a moment, he was back with her glass and the milk. He poured for her, then sat again, pulling his chair closer.

"Chloe asleep?"

Dani shook her head. "No, but she's on her way. She got kind of riled up there."

"Who could blame her."

Dani took a cookie and dunked. "Can you believe those women?"

"It was pretty surreal, wasn't it?"

"That's a good way of putting it. What were they expecting? It reminds me of Cinderella. With all the sisters coming over here to try on the glass slipper."

"It won't fit," he said. He caught her gaze just as she was bringing a soggy cookie to her mouth. "Cinderella is already in the house."

She put the cookie down. "Don't," she said. "I don't want to hear that."

"What? That I think you're special?"

"We both know you can be smooth. That you know how to use those pretty words. And we also both know that I'm not going there. So you needn't bother."

"Ouch," he said. "Hold on a second while I pull the knife from my heart."

She shook her head. "Oh, don't be so melodramatic. You'll get over it. Trust me."

"How do you know?"

"Call it a hunch. But I have the feeling you won't be lacking for prom dates once you hit Manhattan."

"Who *did* you go to the prom with?" he asked, figuring a different tactic was called for. But also, oddly, curious.

Dani picked up her cookie again and chewed thoughtfully before she answered. Alex didn't bother with the dunking. He just opened the cookie and ate the good part.

"I went with Randy, the Wonder Jock."

"The guy what's-her-name mentioned?"

"The very one."

"So he's your memory?"

Dani nodded. "Yep."

"Want to tell me?"

She shook her head. "Nope."

"I'm wounded. I thought we were so close."

"We've known each other one day, Mr. Bradley. One very interesting day, but one, nonetheless."

"Hmm. Well, it doesn't make me any less curious."

"You'll survive."

"You sure do have a lot of confidence in me." He grabbed several more cookies and opened them up. He put the sides without the cream back into the bag. "I'll get over it. I'll survive."

"You won't survive if you do that again."

"What?"

She nodded toward the Oreo bag.

"Oh, damn." He reached over and got his cookie halves. "Sorry. I'm not used to sharing."

"I'll let it pass. This time."

"Oh?" He lifted his brow. "Now what exactly would be the punishment for a crime of this magnitude?"

She grinned. Dammit.

"Laundry duty. Definitely."

"That's not so bad."

"Have you ever done laundry?"

"Yes, of course. Well, no. Kind of."

"What does that mean?"

"I took my clothes to the fluff-and-fold in college."

She laughed. He felt himself flush. Why should he care about something like dirty linens? But he did.

"That doesn't count, Alex. Sheesh. Fluff-and-fold."

He thought about it for a moment, then he took

his empty cookie halves and very deliberately put them back into the bag. "Well?"

"You realize what you're getting yourself into?"

He nodded. He also remembered what she'd said earlier this evening. About how she had no time. He was only going to be here a few days, and he didn't want her to come home from the clinic and do chores. He wanted her to spend that time with him. So how hard could laundry be?

"Okay. I'll show you the laundry room in the morning before I leave. I warn you, though. You're not going to like it."

"I'll survive," he said. "I might even get over it."

She looked at him quizzically. "You're not at all what I expected."

"What did you expect?"

She sighed. "I expected dry clean only. And now I find you're fluff-and-fold."

"Who knows. Maybe I'll turn out to be just plain wash-and-wear."

"Nah. That doesn't seem likely."

"I might surprise you."

Her grin changed her face once more. Lit it up from the inside out. "Yeah, you just might."

DANI HEARD HIM WALKING. He was upstairs, in the guest room, and she was downstairs in her bathroom. But she heard his footsteps on the wood floor. She'd thought he'd turned in. It had been quiet for almost ten minutes. He probably just needed a glass of water.

She wondered if he wore pajamas, or if he went to bed in the buff. It was easier and less stressful to imagine him in the pjs. Silk ones. Navy blue. Maybe just the bottoms. Riding low on his hips so she would see that line of hair men had that ran from their belly buttons down. She liked that line. A lot.

She turned on the water in the sink and opened up her jar of cold cream. It was still hard to get over the fact that Alex Bradley was sleeping in her house. She'd seen him on ''Entertainment Tonight,'' ''E!'' and even ''Oprah.'' He knew movie stars, presidents and kings. He ate in restaurants they wouldn't let her walk near. He shopped in Neiman Marcus and Barneys, while she went to J.C. Penneys.

On the other hand, he ate the cream side of his Oreo and left the rest. If he laughed too hard, his face scrunched up and he cried real tears. He wasn't above an emergency goldfish rescue.

Why on earth wasn't she up with him right now? She rubbed the cold cream over her face and wetted her washcloth. Was she nuts? It wasn't as if she was a virgin. She was a full grown adult, and she understood exactly where sex fit into the scheme of things. Lots of people had sex because they wanted sex. She'd never thought any less of them. What consenting adults did in the privacy of their homes was perfectly all right with her. She had nothing morally against sleeping with a man out of wedlock. She had even recommended that course for a couple of her women friends.

She washed her face for a while, wondering if he was still walking around. Wondering what he was thinking. He'd said some awfully flattering things tonight. Were any of them true?

The problem was, she didn't trust her own instincts. She'd believed every pretty word Randy had told her, only to find out that he'd lied about everything but the color of the sky. She'd been a fool with him, and it had cost her a great deal. Of course, it had also given her Chloe, which she wouldn't trade for the world, but emotionally, the penalty had been high.

And then, after Randy, there had been Doug. The opposite of Randy in every way. She'd thought she'd finally found someone she could trust. But then his wife had called her that lovely and unforgettable afternoon, and that relationship had blown up in her face. The terrible thing was, she'd never dreamed Doug had lied to her, either. She'd just taken what he said at face value.

Now, faces had very little value. Words were suspect. Motivations were mysteries and intentions were dubious. It wasn't just her heart at stake, either. It was her job to protect Chloe, to make sure that she didn't get hurt.

So how could she trust a man like Alex Bradley

who was used to using words as a tool to get what he wanted? The man had negotiation down to a science, and what was negotiation but manipulation?

No, it was much better to be safe than sorry. She'd stick to her guns and keep her distance. Besides, even if every word the man said were true, he was still leaving in a few days. He'd forget about her the moment he got to Albuquerque. She, on the other hand, doubted she'd forget him...ever.

She finished rinsing her face then put on night cream, brushed her teeth and hair and turned off the light in the bathroom. A creak above her made her still, but although she listened for a long time, she didn't hear anything else. He was probably fast asleep. Dreaming of famous beauties and champagne.

ALEX FIGURED HE WOULD never get to sleep. He'd just lie awake all night, thinking of Dani. There were worse things. Although few less frustrating.

What was it about her? He'd already determined it wasn't her looks. She was pretty, sure, but not devastatingly so. No, this wasn't physical, or maybe it was. Chemical. He felt zapped.

He thought about an old cartoon series from his childhood. Li'l Abner. The wonderfully drawn Stupefyin' Jones had helped him enter puberty in her own comic book fashion. All she'd had to do was look at a man and he was stupefied. That's what

Dani had done to him. He'd been zapped by her magic rays and now he was sunk. Because he didn't want to get her in bed. Well, of course he did, but not just get her in bed. He wanted much more from her. The more didn't have anything specific around it. Just more. But he couldn't have that, could he?

On the other hand, he'd never been one to let no stand in the way. Maybe there was some negotiating room here. He'd gone to the mat with some pretty tough customers, and come out ahead. Something told him Dani would make Donald Trump look like a pussycat, but what the hell. There was nothing to lose. The problem was, he wasn't exactly sure what he wanted from her. Marriage wasn't a good option.

Despite his misgivings, he believed his father's rules made some very legitimate points. The Bradley men had done well for many generations, and they'd all adhered to those same rules. But Dani as a mistress? Jeez, he didn't even like the sound of the word where Dani was concerned. And of course, there was Chloe to think about.

Living in New York would be a plus for the little girl. She could get the education she deserved. He could set Dani up in a practice. They'd live very well; he'd make sure of that. Chloe would get into any college she wanted. Dani could shop at her leisure, have a maid, a cook. It wasn't such a bad package.

The other problem was time. How was he going

to convince her that he was serious with only a few days to play with? Well, he'd just have to figure that out.

Now, if he could just get to sleep. He had to be up with Dani in the morning. Laundry. Damn. Ted would have a heart attack.

THE ALARM WOKE DANI, and she groaned as she reached to turn off the horrifying squeal. She wondered if she'd slept an hour all night. Or even ten minutes. It was Alex, of course, that had kept her awake. Thoughts of him. Dressed. Undressed. Smiling. Kissing. *Kissing*. That was the killer. If she'd never kissed him, things probably would have been fine. But no. He had to go and kiss her and remind her that she had a body and it had needs and he was a man and she was a woman and they both had different parts that meshed so well together.

She hauled herself out of bed and tried not to gasp at her image in the mirror. Thank heavens for makeup. She needed it today.

Her shower was a quick one, and she had to consciously slow herself down when applying that much-needed makeup. But she kept speeding up— her actions and her heart. All because he was here. He was awake. He was Alex.

What in the world was she thinking?

She tried on four different outfits, and finally settled on a pale pink skirt and blouse. She found her pumps, slipped them on, then did a final mirror check. Good thing, too, because she'd forgotten to do her hair, which stuck out all over her head as if she'd been given an electric jolt.

She sighed, and went back to the bathroom. She had this awful feeling today was going to be very, very long.

When she finally made it out of her bedroom, Chloe and Alex were already in the kitchen. She heard Chloe laugh, and that made her smile. Chloe didn't often do that, especially with strangers. Her daughter was always thinking too much to laugh freely. What had Alex said to her?

"Guess what, Mom," Chloe said. "Alex doesn't know how to make toast. Can you believe it?"

Dani looked from her daughter to Alex. He was so beautiful it took her a moment to adjust. It was him, and he was here, and she hadn't just dreamed it all. Right now, he had a very silly grin on his face. A stunning, silly, intimate grin.

"I do know how to use a toaster," he said, nudging Chloe gently with his elbow. "I'm just not familiar with the intricacies of cinnamon toast."

Chloe laughed again, making Dani's heart even fuller. "It doesn't take a rocket scientist, you know."

"Chloe. Be polite. It's not his fault that he doesn't know the first thing about cooking."

"Hey," Alex said. "I made the coffee."

She looked at the counter where he pointed. He'd found an old jar of instant coffee in the cupboard, and had turned on the electric kettle. Which sat right next to the coffeemaker she used every day. "Thank you," she said, smiling.

The kettle hissed then, and Alex poured the boiling water into two cups. "Cream? Sugar?" he asked. He was so inordinately proud of himself, she knew she couldn't keep it together. Her laughter was right there, and one more word from him and she wouldn't be able to hold back.

"I'll get it," she said, hoping he didn't hear the strain in her voice. She quickly opened the fridge, but she didn't get the cream right away. Instead she breathed deeply, forcing herself to think of anything but Alex's face and the hot water. The man was tickled pink that he could plug in a kettle. When they talked about men being from Mars, they had to mean him. A grown man, for heaven's sake. It was too much. What on earth would she do with someone like that?

"Do you have to milk the cow?"

She grabbed the cream and turned to face him.

She caught Alex looking at Chloe. His smile was still there, but now it was totally unconscious. His eyes were narrowed a bit as he studied her daughter, who was busy mixing sugar and cinnamon together in a bowl. Alex's expression was one she was familiar with. She had it herself so often. Wonder. A little confusion. Amazement. Chloe was a unique creature. An incredibly huge brain in such a tiny little thing. So pretty, and so innocent. Dani could tell Alex was seeing all of that. Maybe more.

He turned from Chloe and focused that same intense gaze on her. Dani felt the first flush of the morning on her cheeks. How he did that to her was still a mystery. She didn't look away, though. When his smile broadened she saw it. When the look of wonder didn't go away, but instead grew deeper, she saw that, too.

But mostly, she saw his desire. In the light of day, it was unmistakable. No errant shadow, no trick of the moon. He wanted her in a way that was real and tangible and spoke the question as loudly as words.

She wondered if he could see just as clearly that her response was, "Yes."

"Laundry," he said, his voice gravelly and rough.

"Fluff-and-fold," she whispered back.

His grin grew mischievous. "Wash-and-wear."

"You guys are weird," Chloe said. Then she took her cinnamon toast to the table, shaking her head all the way.

Chapter Eight

"Are you sure you want to do this?"

Alex looked at the neat piles of sorted laundry in the small pantry off the kitchen. Then he looked at his notes. "Yep. I lost fair and square. The laundry will be done."

"Okay. But you don't have to."

"I know. I want to."

She looked up at him with an achingly sweet smile, and he realized that although it was a piddly task, one that meant nothing in the overall scheme of things, he really wanted to do it for her. To do it well. He wanted her to come home to perfectly folded towels and socks and shake her head and tell him she was impressed and pleased. It was also true that he could tell her quite a few tales of his financial and corporate efforts that were a hell of a lot more impressive than separating whites from darks, but right now, it was the laundry he needed to conquer.

"Feel free to use the phone," she said. "And eat

whatever you like. I'll come home about one for lunch.''

"Do you want me to fix you something?" he asked.

Her grin broadened. "No, I think you're going to have your hands full today. I'll bring something back with me. Then, maybe you could come back to the clinic with me to see Pete.''

"Great. I'd like that.''

She really was beautiful. Standing so close to her in the small room was getting to be a little difficult. He kept wanting to touch her. To feel her skin and her hair. To kiss her. God, yes. Kiss her.

The moment stretched. If it were another woman, he wouldn't have hesitated. He would have swept her into his arms and kissed her till they both cried uncle. But with Dani he found himself hesitating. She wasn't like other women. She needed deft handling, consideration and patience. He was pretty sure he could manage the first two, but patience? There was no time for a long courtship. There was barely time for any courtship at all. No, he had to let her know. Now.

He leaned forward. She closed her eyes and leaned, too, and he felt immediate relief, and excitement. To know she wanted the same thing he did...at least for now.

Just as his lips touched hers, Chloe opened the door.

"I'm late for—"

Alex jerked back. So did Dani. He picked up the box of Tide and read the back furiously, his face hot with embarrassment. Although why he felt this way was not clear. He hadn't done anything. Even if the kiss had been completed, there was still no reason to blush.

"I know, honey. We're almost done here. Get your lunch and meet me at the front door."

"Were you two kissing?"

Alex chanced a look at Dani. Her face was as red as his must have been, but other than that, she looked remarkably composed. Especially after that question.

"Yes, we were. Or, we were going to."

"Why?"

"Because grown-up friends sometimes kiss," Dani said.

She wouldn't look at him. He went back to reading about tough stains.

"I don't care, you know," Chloe said, the censure clear in her voice. "You can kiss all you want. But I'd prefer you did it when I wasn't late for school."

He coughed. Well, choked. He heard Dani clear her throat. The presoak instructions held his rapt attention. Dani, however, got it in gear. She walked toward the door, then stopped.

"I'll call you as soon as I check on Pete," she said. "And don't forget to dry the sweaters on the rack."

He dared a glance and was rewarded with a guilty little smile. It would do till she got home. "Yes, ma'am. I'll do my best."

Then Chloe grabbed Dani's hand and pulled her away.

"Don't forget the cat," he called out, not wanting to deal with that particular feline all day.

"Right!"

He listened for a while. Chloe's entreaties got more urgent. The cat hissed. Dani was patient and never raised her voice. Finally he heard the front door close. He was alone. With the laundry. Have mercy.

SHE COULDN'T CONCENTRATE. Dani petted the pregnant dachshund on the exam table and forced herself yet again to banish Alex from her thoughts. The pup was actually in good shape. It was her owner that needed calming. Thank goodness there hadn't been any real emergencies today. Just routine exams, a couple of shots and of course, Pete.

Alex's dog was improving, although not quite as quickly as she'd have liked. She would keep him on the IV for another twenty-four hours. On the other hand, his appetite was picking up, and that was a good sign.

It occurred to her that while she wasn't happy that Pete was still not up to par, she was glad that Alex would have to stay for at least one, probably two more days. Just the thought of him in her

house, waiting for her, was enough to make her
pulse speed up.

That she was so pleased annoyed her. She knew
full well that the longer Alex stayed the worse it
was going to be when he left. She already liked
him too much. And she wanted to believe him too
much. He made it so easy, with his convincing
words and his expressive eyes.

"Well?"

Dani jerked away from her thoughts of Alex and
realized she'd been staring at Edna Bickle for who
knows how long, while Tinkle, her unfortunately
named dachshund, was flat on her back while Dani
rubbed her tummy.

Dani stilled her hand and continued her examination, flustered that she was so unable to control
herself. This time, she made it through, gave Edna
the good news that Tinkle was the picture of health
and sent dog and owner off. All of it without thinking of Alex even once.

It was 12:10 and she had one more patient to see:
a kitten who needed her shots. If she hurried, she
could be done in about five minutes, and then she
could head over to the diner, pick up lunch, then
be home at 12:45. She hurried.

AT 12:45, DANI OPENED her front door. The first
thing she heard was laughter. Female laughter.

Dani walked quickly toward the kitchen and put
the bag of turkey sandwiches on the table. Again,

the sound of feminine laughter assailed her, and it was no TV or radio program. That was a woman. Here. In her house. With Alex.

As she headed toward the laundry room, she heard it again, only this time, more than one voice pealed in glee. She felt her temperature rise and her adrenaline kick in. Who had he brought here?

Dani turned the corner and stood at the door to her pantry. Alex was too busy to notice her arrival. Too busy with three women, all of whom she knew, all of whom were supposedly friends of hers, and one of whom had a pair of Dani's bikini panties in the air, twirling it around, which Alex tried to grab by getting very, very close. To make matters worse, her washing machine was open, and suds, *lots* of suds spilled out of the top, down the sides, onto the floor and into the still-waiting piles of laundry.

Crystal Crane, the woman with the panties held aloft, was leaning back over the dryer. Her crop-top T-shirt was pulled so high that Dani could see the undersides of her nonbra-clad breasts. One more inch, and she'd be fully exposed. Dani held her breath as Alex reached higher…then he stopped. Leaned back. Put his hand down.

"You win," he said. "You can keep them."

Crystal didn't move. She knew what position she was in, and she had no qualms about how sugges-tive she was. "Come on, Alex. Don't be such a party pooper."

"This isn't a party," he said, his voice quite firm.

"And I appreciate you ladies trying to help, but I've got things under control now."

"Do you really?" Dani said.

Four pairs of eyes turned to her. All extremely wide.

"Dani," Alex said.

"Dani" came the Greek chorus.

"Yes," she said, folding her arms across her chest. "Dani. Whose house this is."

Crystal finally pulled her hand down. She didn't let go of the panties, though, she just put her hand behind her back. "We came over to ask Alex—"

"If he wanted to be—" Karen Stovall said, interrupting.

"Part of the opening ceremonies—" Jean Crocket added, butting in.

"This weekend," Crystal finished.

"He won't be staying that long," Dani said. She turned her gaze to Alex then, and got some tiny bit of satisfaction that he looked exceedingly guilty. "Pete will be on his feet by Friday."

"That's great," he said. "But..."

"But he already said yes," Crystal said. "Didn't you, Alex?"

Alex didn't look at Crystal. But he did nod. "That I did."

"He's going to take pictures with people," Jean said. "And sign autographs. With him there, I'll bet we can get TV coverage from Albuquerque. Maybe even national coverage."

"We'll get more people here than we ever dreamed," Karen said. "Imagine. The Sexiest Man in the World right here in Carlson's Gap. We'll raise a fortune."

"National coverage," Dani said, her heart sinking as if it were a stone. "I see." She did, too. All that talk about how he didn't want the publicity was just that. Talk. The first chance he got to flaunt his fame, and he leapt at it as a starving dog leaps at a bone. "Mind telling me what happened to that?" She pointed to the washer.

"Oh, I think that was my fault," Jean said. "I guess he'd already added the detergent."

"No, I added the detergent," Karen said, holding up her hand as if she were a guilty schoolgirl.

"Uh-oh," Crystal said. "I did, too."

"Swell," Dani said.

"We'll pay for any repairs," Crystal said, moving now toward the door, and escape. "Won't we?"

"Of course," Karen said, picking up the cue and moving, too.

"Right," Jean added.

Then the three women walked past her, fast, and were on their way out. No one bothered to say goodbye. Alex hadn't moved.

"I can explain," he said.

"No need. I understand completely."

"I don't think you do."

He pointed to a folded stack of towels on the counter. "I got the one batch done just fine."

"I told you, you don't need to explain. Besides, I'm late. I brought you a turkey sandwich. I'd appreciate it if you could call the repair service. I can't afford to be without the machine for long. The number is right there on the side."

"Wait a minute. Weren't you here to have lunch with me?"

"That was the plan. But plans change. I have to get back to work."

He moved toward her, and she stepped back.

"Look, I didn't ask them to do this," he said. "I really was doing fine before they showed up."

"You don't owe me any explanations. Just please get the washer fixed." She turned, anxious to get away. Even as she felt it, she knew her disappointment was silly. Hadn't she known all along who he was? That whatever he said was bound to be some kind of a lie?

"Wait."

She stopped.

"Don't go. I don't want to leave it like this."

She turned once more to face him. "Like what?"

"You're angry."

"No, I'm not."

"Please stay. You don't have to. But I'd appreciate it. I didn't know they were going to come in here and mess with your things. If I had, I would never have opened the door. I thought they were your friends."

"I thought so, too."

"For what it's worth, I don't think they meant any harm."

"Of course not. Look, forget it. It's fine. Really. I just have to get back—"

He was in front of her somehow, with his hands on her arms. Standing close. Looking down into her eyes. "You can't think I wanted this to turn out badly."

She couldn't look back at him. Not at those pleading eyes. If she did, she would start believing him again. "Let me go please."

"Not till you look at me."

"Alex, stop it."

He let go with his right arm, and raised his fingers to her chin. He lifted her head up until she was forced to meet his gaze. "Please, Dani."

She wanted to believe his eyes. That was the whole problem. He looked so sincere, as if it mattered to him that she was upset, that he'd upset her.

"I wanted so much to do this one thing for you," he said. "And I've screwed it up royally. Give me another chance?"

"What for?" she said, hating to say the words, but knowing she had to. "You're a guest. A visitor. You don't have to do anything to impress me."

"I'm not trying to impress you." He shook his head. "No, that's not true. I am. But not the way you mean it. I know it sounds stupid, but I wanted to make things easier for you today. To take care

of this damn laundry so you wouldn't have to. I
thought it was going to be a piece of cake.''

"Most things aren't. At least, not for me. I imagine you're pretty used to seeing things go your
way.''

"Dani, just because I have some money doesn't
mean the world bows down in front of me. I have
my own struggles.''

She felt a stab of guilt. Of course he had his
struggles. They were just worlds away from her
own. "I'm sorry. I really didn't mean that as a put-
down.''

"Those women, I...''

"I understand.''

"Do you?'' he said, taking hold of her arms once
again. "I thought they were friends. They said—''

"I can imagine what they said. The women in
this town aren't going to let up, you know. They're
going to keep traipsing over here, trying to get your
attention. You're big news in a town this size.''

"I wish more than ever they'd never run that
stupid article.''

"Do you? Really?''

"Now what's that supposed to mean?''

"I think you might be enjoying some of this no-
toriety, that's all. And who could blame you? It's
got to be a thrill to know the world looks at you as
the sexiest man alive.''

"How do *you* look at me?''

She paused, terribly conscious of his hands on

PLAY HARLEQUIN'S

LUCKY HEARTS
GAME

AND YOU GET

- ◆ **FREE BOOKS!**
- ◆ **A FREE GIFT!**
- ◆ **AND MUCH MORE!**

TURN THE PAGE AND DEAL YOURSELF IN...

Play "Lucky Hearts" for this...

exciting FREE gift!
This surprise
mystery gift could
be yours free

when you play **LUCKY HEARTS!**

**...then continue your lucky streak
with a sweetheart of a deal!**

1. Play Lucky Hearts as instructed on the opposite page.

2. Send back this card and you'll receive brand-new Harlequin American Romance® novels. These books have a cover price of $3.99 each, but they are yours to keep absolutely free

3. There's no catch. You're under no obligation to buy anything. We charge nothing — ZERO — for your first shipment. And you don't have to make any minimum number of purchases — not even one!

4. The fact is thousands of readers enjoy receiving books by mail from the Harlequin Reader Service™. They like the convenience of home delivery... they like getting the best new novels BEFORE they're available in stores... and they love our discount prices!

5. We hope that after receiving your free books you'll want to remain a subscriber. But the choice is yours — to continue or cancel, any time at all! So why not take us up on our invitation, with no risk of any kind. You'll be glad you did!

©1996 HARLEQUIN ENTERPRISES LTD.

The Harlequin Reader Service® — Here's how it works:

Accepting free books places you under no obligation to buy anything. You may keep the books and gift and return the shipping statement marked "cancel." If you do not cancel, about a month later we'll send you 4 additional novels and bill you just $3.34 each plus 25¢ delivery per book and applicable sales tax, if any.* That's the complete price — and compared to cover prices of $3.99 each — quite a bargain! You may cancel at any time, but if you choose to continue, every month we'll send you 4 more books, which you may either purchase at the discount price... or return to us and cancel your subscription.

*Terms and prices subject to change without notice. Sales tax applicable in N.Y.

If offer card is missing write to: Harlequin Reader Service, 3010 Walden Ave., P.O. Box 1867, Buffalo, NY 14240-1867

BUSINESS REPLY MAIL
FIRST-CLASS MAIL   PERMIT NO. 717   BUFFALO, NY

POSTAGE WILL BE PAID BY ADDRESSEE

HARLEQUIN READER SERVICE
3010 WALDEN AVE
PO BOX 1867
BUFFALO NY 14240-9952

NO POSTAGE
NECESSARY
IF MAILED
IN THE
UNITED STATES

her arms. The heat from his skin went right through the material of her blouse, and coursed up and down her body as if it were an electrical charge. "I can see how they came to anoint you."

He smiled for the first time since she'd been home. "Does that mean what I hope it means?"

"I don't know. What are you hoping for?"

"That you find me half as sexy as I find you."

She closed her eyes. He'd almost had her. "Alex, please..."

"God, what? Why are you looking at me like that? Can't you see I mean what I say? I find you incredibly sexy, Dani Jacobson. I didn't get any sleep last night, just thinking about you downstairs. I haven't called my office. I haven't even asked about Pete. All I can think of is you."

"Don't do this to me!" She pulled herself away from him. "Is this some kind of game you've invented? Torment the poor country girl? Let her imagine that you're really interested, when it's completely clear to anyone with half a brain that you couldn't possibly be? Well, it's not funny. And more than that, it's not nice. So cut it out, will you? Just cut it out."

She turned quickly and headed toward the front door. All she wanted was to be away from him. But he caught her and held her still. Forced her to turn around again. To look up at his wounded gaze.

"I'm not doing that, Dani. Dammit. I wouldn't do a thing like that."

"How do I know? I don't know you at all."

"Yes, you do. Or you could. If you'd let yourself. I've done nothing but tell you the truth since we met. And I'm not lying now."

"Just like you weren't lying about being the Sexiest Man in the World?"

His brows came together. "What are you talking about?"

"Oh, please. You were awfully quick to say you'd stay for the weekend."

"Of course. What does that have to do with anything?"

"You like the attention. You like the women slobbering over you. Don't deny it. Why else would you agree to stick around this Podunk town? What could you possibly want here?"

"You."

"Stop it."

"I won't. Not until you listen to me."

"You think I'd ask you to take pictures and sign autographs?"

"No, you wouldn't but your friends did. So I said yes."

"Well, you shouldn't have."

"Why? Why is this such a bad thing, Dani? Tell me."

"No. Just please leave me alone, would you? You can stay here for Pete's sake, but I think it's best that we stay clear of each other."

"No."

"What do you mean, no? I'm asking you politely to leave me be."

"I can't."

"Sure you can. And you will. Come the weekend, you'll be on your way to New York. I'll be some fading memory. It's really quite simple."

"That's where you're wrong. There's nothing simple about you."

She shook her head. "Look, I'll call the repairman. You don't have to. I'll just call from the clinic." She walked toward the door again. Determined this time to leave, no matter what he said or did.

"Dani!"

She didn't stop. She wouldn't, not for anything. There was nothing he could say that would make the outcome any different. But if she stayed, if she listened to him, she'd just get hurt much, much worse.

"Dani, don't go."

She turned the handle.

"Dammit, stop."

She opened the door.

"Dani, I want you to come to New York with me. You and Chloe."

Chapter Nine

Dani couldn't move. Her hand froze on the door-knob. "What did you say?"

"I said I want you and Chloe to come with me to New York."

Against her better judgment, she turned. She expected to see him laughing at his colossal joke. But he wasn't. "You can't be serious," she said.

"I am."

"We've known each other two days."

"Sometimes two days is enough."

"Enough?"

He nodded and walked slowly toward her. "Enough to know that this isn't ordinary attraction. There's more going on here, Dani, and you know it."

"I don't believe that."

"Only because you don't want to." He was very close to her now. He reached behind her and pushed the front door closed.

She had to look up to see his face. What she

didn't understand was her reaction to his absurd suggestion. Her pulse raced, her heart thudded in her chest. She could feel the excitement as if it were a living thing inside her.

"You can't deny it," he said, his voice a whisper. "You can't tell me you don't feel this thing between us. This pull. I see it in your eyes, Dani. We both know something very strong is happening."

"I can't," she said.

"Why not?"

"Because I don't believe you."

"I'd never hurt you."

"Yes, you would. You wouldn't mean to. It wouldn't start out that way. But you would."

"No."

"I'm okay for New Mexico, but not for New York. If you think about it for even a minute, you'll see that."

"Why do you do that?"

"What?"

"Put yourself down like that."

"I'm not." He was too close to her. It was hard to think straight when she could feel his heat. "I'm just being realistic."

"Don't you realize I've been to New York before? And Paris and Los Angeles and all over the damn world. I've seen what's out there. And what's right here. And I want you."

"Why?"

He looked at her with those eyes of his, and she could feel her resolve weakening. It was stupid, childish to listen to him. To think he could be serious. But then he moved those last few inches, and his kiss wiped logic clear away.

Alex took refuge in the kiss. He'd stunned himself with his words. He hadn't had any idea he wanted Dani so much, or that he would blurt it out so plainly. She obviously took his finesse away as well as his breath. But thinking would have to come later. Now, all he wanted was to float away with her kiss.

Her lips were so giving, her tongue so eager. Her responsiveness worked him up in a heartbeat. When she moved her hips closer, rubbing against him, he was sure she could tell what she did to him. There was an innocence to her, mixed with a heat that was undeniable. That's what it was, of course. The intriguing blend that made Dani who she was. She was intelligent, but hadn't lost her childlike sense of fun. She was beautiful, but didn't use it to manipulate. Sensuous, yet guileless. As strong as steel and as soft as velvet. He wanted her so badly it scared him.

She pulled back, and he could see the flush on her cheeks. Her lips were still parted and inviting, and he had to force himself not to take her into his arms again. But he'd already pushed too hard. He didn't think he'd blown it, but he'd come close.

"You didn't answer my question," Dani said, taking yet another step back.

"What question?"

"Why?"

He smiled. She really didn't get it. Didn't believe him. Well, why should she? He barely believed it himself. "Because," he said, trying to figure out his answer even as he spoke. "Because you've done something to me. I can't explain it. All I know is I can't stop thinking about you. There's something strong going on between us, and I don't want to just leave it here. I don't think that would be fair to either of us."

She glanced down, then back up at him, although he could see it wasn't easy for her. She wanted to run, and there was a part of him that wanted her to. Life had been a lot simpler just a little over a day ago. Boring, maybe, but simpler.

"I'll admit something is going on between us," she said. "But I think it's pretty basic. We're attracted to each other. Physically. It's nothing more than hormones at work."

He shook his head. "That would be easier, but you know it's not true."

"No, I don't know that. I don't know what to think. I've known you only a day, and you're asking me to come to New York and be your mistress. How is that supposed to make sense?"

"Who said anything about being a mistress?"

She blinked. "You mean that was a proposal?"

"Well, no. Not exactly."

"Then what, exactly?"

This wasn't going well. He'd said too much without thinking things through, which wasn't like him at all. The reason he was so successful in business was that he'd been trained for logic. To extrapolate, to consider all sides. And here he was blundering around like a fool. "I don't know," he said, opting for honesty. "Maybe we just need time to figure that out."

"And what if you figure out that it's all been a mistake? That it was, in fact, just hormones? What then?"

"That wouldn't happen."

She laughed. "No? Your crystal ball is that good?"

He shook his head. "No. But my instincts are telling me that we can't drop this here, Dani. I've learned to trust my instincts."

"I have, too, Alex. And mine are on full alert. You'll forgive me if I don't believe the fairy tale. But in my experience, no one really lives happily ever after."

"Maybe your experience is about to change."

She sighed. It was a hard sound to listen to, so filled with resignation.

"We'll never know. I've really got to get back to work. You can come and see Pete if you like."

"I want to get that washer fixed."

"Oh, yeah. Thanks. But after that, why don't you

come by? Mimi will be here at three to wait for Chloe.''

He nodded. "Okay. But Dani?"

"Hmm?"

"Just think about it? Please? Don't just dismiss me out of hand."

Her lips came together and her brows came down, but only for a second. "All right. I will. But you have to promise to think about it, too. Not just the romantic side to this, but the practical side. The wash-and-wear side."

He smiled. "It's a deal." But as she walked away, his smile faltered. She seemed so in control. So certain of her reactions. Yet he was behaving as if he were a schoolboy. Then he noticed she'd left her purse sitting on the counter. Maybe she wasn't so certain after all.

"YOO-HOO! MR. BRADLEY!"

Alex stopped at the sound of his name and looked around to see who was calling him. He knew he was on the right street to find Dani's clinic, but he didn't remember how far he had to go to get there. He'd just passed the ice-cream parlor, and was now in front of a dry cleaner's. Behind him, he saw a woman waving and hurrying toward him. He couldn't tell if this was one of the women he'd met before, or someone new.

As she got closer, he could make out the details of her face. Middle-aged, brown hair in a sort of pageboy, no makeup, friendly smile. Nope, this was someone he hadn't met.

She reached him, but didn't say anything for a minute. She just gave him a warm smile as she caught her breath. He smiled back, wondering if it was an autograph she wanted, or something more.

"Thanks for stopping," she said, still sounding a bit breathless.

"No problem."

"I just wanted to say thank you."

"For what?"

She shifted her heavy-looking purse from one shoulder to the other. Like Dani, this woman seemed to be a real person. No impossibly high heels or tight dress or bare midriff. Just jeans and a T-shirt.

"For agreeing to come to the Main Street festival."

"Is that what I agreed to do? I never did hear the details."

"Yep, that's it. We're trying to bring trade back to Main Street. It's been over five years in the planning, and now, we're ready to roll. Dani didn't tell you?"

He shook his head. "She's been a little busy."

"Hmm. Nobody should be that busy. I'm Laura Phelps, by the way. Dani's aunt."

He stuck out his hand and she grabbed it. The shake was friendly and warm, like her smile. "Pleasure."

She laughed. "I'll bet. This place must seem like Dullsville to you, huh?"

"Not at all. It's been pretty lively since I arrived."

"I've heard about all your company," she said, raising her brows meaningfully. "Don't judge us all by a few silly women. Most of us here are salt-of-the-earth folk. Not glamorous by any stretch, but basically honest and good."

"That beats glamorous any day."

She nodded, but at the same time she was busy taking him in. Her intelligent gaze swept over him slowly from head to toe. Funny, he wanted her to approve. She was Dani's aunt after all. Perhaps a good word from her would go far.

"You know that half the proceeds from the festival are earmarked for Dani's animal shelter?"

"Karen mentioned something about that."

"With you on board, that's going to turn out to be quite a bit of money, I'm thinking."

"I don't know. I don't think salt-of-the-earth folks give too big a damn about someone like me."

Her smile widened. "Even us salty types like a little celebrity spice now and then. We'll get us a turnout. You just watch."

"Well, I'm glad to help."

"That shelter means a heck of a lot to our girl."

He folded his arms over his chest and studied her for a moment. Something was going on, and it only took him a few more seconds to get it. "So what's the overall budget of this shelter?" he asked.

"Around one hundred thousand."

"And what do you expect to earn at this festival?"

"With you there? Maybe ten thousand. Maybe a little less."

He nodded. "I assume you'd take anonymous donations?"

Her smile was relieved, and pleased. "You betcha."

"I mean it about the anonymous part."

She crossed her heart with her index finger. "I'll never tell a soul."

"It's a deal."

"Um, mind telling me what this donation is going to be?"

He grinned. "I really hope you're in sales. It would be a pity to waste your talent."

"Real estate. Number one in the county."

"Uh-huh. Well, Aunt Laura, you can put me down for the balance."

Her eyes widened. "You sure? That's quite a chunk of change."

"I can write it off."

"Hot damn," she said, rubbing her hands together. "I like your style."

"Yours isn't too bad, either," he said.

She winked at him. "Number one in the county.

Well, I've kept you long enough. I'll be sure and find you on Saturday.''

"I figured.''

"You be good now,'' she said cheerfully. Then she moved off, but before she got too far away she stopped and turned to face him. "A lot of people here love Dani, you know.''

"That's no surprise.''

"We care what happens to her.''

"Uh-huh.''

"As nice as you've been, I don't think there's anything to worry about, but you just remember. This is her home. Her town. She's one of our own.''

"I have no intention of hurting her,'' he said.

"Good.'' She turned once more but only got one step away before she stopped again. "Alex?''

He nodded.

"It's been a long time between boyfriends, you know.''

His eyes narrowed. What was she getting at? "Yes?''

"I'm thinking it wouldn't do either of you any harm to do some smooching.''

He grinned. "I like the way you think.''

"Smooching, bucko. That's all. You want to do more, you'd better be looking at rings.''

"I see.''

"Okay then.'' With that, she turned again and this time he watched her walk all the way down to the bank and go inside.

Looking at rings. Just the mention of the small gold bands had him shaking his head. He wasn't ready for marriage, and Dani... He had made peace with the idea of wanting her beyond reason, but marriage? How could he forget everything he'd ever learned, toss his whole history aside? There hadn't been many hard and fast rules in his life, but the ones that were there were stringent. The kind of woman that equaled success was as clear to him as the bright afternoon sun. She had to be a little timid. Not too bright. Model pretty. A good hostess. A dutiful wife who understood her place in the scheme of things.

Dani was none of those things. Well, nothing except pretty, but even there she wasn't the kind of pretty his father had meant. A sudden thought stopped him. Was he attracted to Dani just because she wasn't his ideal? Was this all an act of rebellion, and not true desire?

He continued to walk toward the clinic, but slowly, thinking. He'd had plenty of time in his life to rebel. Why would he start now? There was much more involved here than making a statement against his father's way of life. If he hadn't seen for himself that the rules worked, that would be one thing. But he had. He'd seen his father's power and success. Seen how his own mother had been part of that success. True, he'd wondered from time to time if his father wouldn't have been happier married to one of his mistresses. But once he'd discovered his mother had a lover of her own, it all made sense.

It was civilized as hell, and no one seemed to get hurt. At least he'd never heard them complain.

Of course he could never have Dani as his mistress. It wouldn't be anything so old-fashioned. Of course he'd help her financially, but that just made sense. The one thing he had plenty of was money. But he'd never expect Dani to stop her practice. To live her life just for his pleasure. He'd encourage her to get the most out of life. To do the things she'd always wanted to. They could be friends, and lovers, and companions. So what if they weren't married? That wasn't so important these days. Besides, she was so independent, she probably didn't even want to marry.

He finally reached the clinic, and pulled open the glass door. Several people were in the waiting room, along with their pets. Two dogs, one a Great Dane, the other a terrier, were busy sniffing each other. A cat, held by a teenage boy with several earrings in his right ear and his nose, meowed loudly. He also saw a bird, a snake in a box and a hamster.

All of the owners, with the exception of the teenage boy, stared at him. It wasn't the usual polite look people gave when a newcomer joined the party, but full-out gawking. He smiled, but his heart wasn't in it. He was in no mood to be a celebrity this afternoon.

Moving to the reception desk, he saw the young woman who'd helped him the other day. She didn't wait for him to ask for admittance. She just went to the door and opened it for him.

"Dani's in with a patient now, but you can go back and see Pete. Last door on the right."

"Thanks," he said, heading back.

He heard her long sigh, and knew without checking that she was watching him. Probably checking out his butt. Oh, well. There was nothing he could do about that.

He turned the corner and entered the large room he'd been in last night. Pete was already on his feet, wagging his whole body. Damn, it felt good to see his old friend looking so good. His coat was shinier than it had been in ages. Even from here, Alex could see his breathing was better.

He went to the cage and opened it up. Pete was on him in a flash, and when Alex sat down, Pete licked his face with such affection Alex laughed out loud. Which wasn't such a smart move. He loved Pete, but not enough to French kiss.

"I think he missed you a little."

Alex looked up to see Dani standing by the door. She looked so beautiful in her white lab coat. Why something so plain should make her look so good was a question for the fashion experts. All he knew was that he wanted her. Right then and there. "I've missed you," he said.

"Well, don't go licking my face to show me,"

she said, walking toward the cage. "He's really doing well. His respiration is back to normal, he's eating. But he's still a little dehydrated."

"Then you want him here for another night?"

She nodded. "It would be best, I think. If he were a little younger I wouldn't be so concerned."

"I don't want to take any risks."

"Good. But you can spring him tomorrow. No reason to keep him here after that."

"Would you mind if I brought him to your place?"

She shook her head. "No. But there's really no need to. It's really not necessary for you to stay over the weekend. I mean, it was nice of you to agree and all, but if you're staying out of some feeling of obligation..."

"I'm not. I want to stay."

"It's going to be a zoo. And you're going to be the prize exhibit."

"I can take it."

"Take it? Or want it?"

He really looked at her then. She wouldn't meet his gaze, and he saw a slight flush on her cheeks. "Dani?"

"Yes?"

"What's this about?"

She still didn't look at him. "Nothing."

"No, you said something earlier, back at the house. Something about me enjoying the attention."

"Don't you?"

He shook his head. "You think I want to stay here because I want a bunch of strange women pawing me?"

"I think that's part of it."

He sighed. "Dani, my sweet. For a smart woman, you can be awfully dumb."

She straightened, and the first look she gave him head-on was full of indignation. "I beg your pardon?"

He stood up and walked over to her. Damn, she made him so crazy. "There's only one thing that could keep me in this town once Pete is well and that's you."

He waited patiently for her to meet his gaze. When she did, her eyes weren't troubled, as he'd anticipated. They were filled with fire.

"So let me ask you something, Mr. I-only-tell-the-truth. If I sleep with you tonight, are you still going to want to stick around tomorrow?"

Chapter Ten

Dani could barely believe she'd asked him the question. His face told her he was having trouble believing it as well. But darn it, she wanted to know. Of course, no matter what his answer was, she would still have her doubts. But maybe there would be a hint of guilt in his eyes, a flash of remorse on his face that would tell her the truth. She studied him intently, but she didn't see a sign of either.

What she did see was hurt. Confusion. Desire.

"You think all I want is to make love to you?" he asked. "Honestly?"

"I think it's a possibility."

He sighed as he studied her. "What we have here is a problem. If we don't have sex, you won't come with me because you'll think I just want to have sex, and that'll be that. But I don't want to have sex just to prove something to you." He stepped closer and brushed the back of his hand against her cheek. "The thing is, I want to make love with you.

That requires two people, both of whom want to share something intimate and special. Not a scientific experiment.''

She melted into his caress. The feel of his hand on her skin made her close her eyes to concentrate. She reached up and held his hand steady, not willing to let him go. "That *is* a problem," she whispered.

"It doesn't have to be."

It was her turn to sigh. And open her eyes. She didn't just let go of his hand, but took it in hers and brought it down to his side. There she left it, although it brought a quick lump to her throat. "Maybe you should just leave tomorrow."

"Is that what you want?"

She almost said yes. She tried to say yes. But the word wouldn't come. "I don't know," she said, finally.

"Here's what I think." He didn't bring his hand to her cheek again. Instead he circled her waist with his arms and pulled her very close against him. His body and hers touched from knee to chest. Her nipples immediately hardened against him, although she didn't think he could feel it. She, however, felt his arousal against her lower belly and the thought of him so hard just from talking about making love with her was enough to make her dizzy.

"I think you don't know me well enough yet," he said. "If you did, the problem would be solved."

His little grin told her he was kidding. Well, almost kidding. She had to concentrate on his grin, because if she thought about her body, or his, this conversation would be moot in about three hot seconds. She swallowed, and hoped her voice wouldn't betray the heat that was coursing through her. "Boy, that's some ego you have there."

"Hey, I promised I'd only tell you the truth. Besides, some information is hard to disguise." He pulled her tighter to prove his point.

Despite the voice inside her head that kept repeating the urgent warning to leave, right now, she brought her arms up and circled his neck. Her ability to speak had fled, and all she could do was look up into those beautiful dark eyes. The confusion and hurt were gone, leaving his desire so plain and clear that it made her stomach clench to see it.

He moved his head down, slowly, while he kept her gaze locked on his. Was her expression a reflection of his own? Could he see how much she wanted him?

When his lips touched hers, she knew he could read her like a book. He was right. Some things couldn't be disguised.

"Dani—oh!"

Dani pulled away from Alex, and stepped back until her heel hit Pete's cage. Connie stood in the doorway. Her startled gaze went from Alex to Dani, and then her expression changed to one of pure amazement. Dani recognized the look. She'd seen it often enough when she'd been with Randy. The unasked question was always there. What would a man like *him* be doing with a woman like *her*. She couldn't blame Connie, though. The question was quite reasonable.

"I'm sorry. I didn't mean to interrupt," Connie said, stepping back.

"It's all right," Dani said, her composure remarkably intact given the circumstances. "What's going on?"

"We're just stacking up out here, is all. You've got patients in three rooms."

"Of course. I'll be right there."

Connie stared at her a moment longer, then let her gaze move to Alex. She sighed, and her lips opened slightly, and Dani could see the young woman's lust as plainly as she could see her pale blue uniform. It occurred to her once more that Alex saw that all the time. Women threw themselves at him on a regular basis. Beautiful women. Young women. Women with huge breasts and long legs and naturally curly blond hair. No man could resist all that. Not even Alex.

"If you don't mind," he said, "I'm going to stay here with Pete for a little while."

She found Alex looking at her, not Connie, even though her niece was still gaping at him. "Stay as long as you like."

"I've got some business to attend to at three, so I'll have to leave pretty soon. Oh, the washer is fixed."

"Great," she said, although at the moment she couldn't have cared less. "Then I'll see you when I get through here."

"Have any idea when that might be?"

"Six or a little after."

He looked briefly toward the door, and she did, too. Connie got the hint and left rather quickly. Then Dani's gaze went back to Alex.

"About our problem," he said. "What do you say we tackle that when you get home. Let me take you somewhere for dinner. Just the two of us. It'll give us a chance to talk."

"What about Chloe?"

"We can sit down with her while she has dinner. I'll make the reservation for eight. Except you'll have to tell me where."

She nodded, very pleased that he was considerate enough to understand that dinner with her daughter was important. "Try the Blue Willow Café. I think you'll like it there."

"The Blue Willow it is," he said.

She started toward the door, trying hard to shift gears. Her patients deserved her full attention. Thinking about Alex would have to wait. For the next few hours she was going to be a vet, not a woman.

She would have, honest, if he hadn't caught her arm, spun her around and kissed her. His lips on hers were soft and firm, urgent and tender. His tongue teased her into opening her mouth, tasting him and letting him taste her. His hands moved beneath her white coat to explore her back, while he brought her body tight against him. She felt him, hard once more, against her stomach. The awareness that she did that to him was as confusing to her as her own reactions. Her hardened nipples, the tightness in her belly, the need to clench her thighs together.

A dog's bark mingled with Alex's moan, and while she wanted to ignore the bark and concentrate on making him moan again, she couldn't. It wasn't easy, but she pulled herself away from his lips and his arms. Before she weakened, she left him standing there, not daring to look back even once.

HAD THERE EVER BEEN a longer afternoon? Dani doubted it. Time had inched by slowly as she'd examined dogs and cats and birds and snakes. Every time she paused, Alex filled her thoughts and she'd had to force herself back to the puppy or kitten. At five, she'd come to the conclusion that the whole system of love and lust was seriously flawed. It was detrimental to the work ethic, and played havoc with the natural order of things. Life had been so much simpler just two days ago. Work and Chloe had filled her life to the brink, and it had been enough. Now, she was overflowing, and that couldn't continue. It just couldn't.

So why was she hurrying so? Why did she have

to fight the urge to run home? To fly into his arms? It wasn't fair. That's all.

She crossed the last street, and forced herself to walk normally toward her house, even though her pulse was elevated and her heart thudded in her chest. The thought of sitting with Alex at the Café, sipping wine, gazing into his eyes was nearly too much to bear. She hadn't felt this excited about her prom. What was he doing to her?

As she approached her house, she saw a very long black stretch limousine parked in front of her next door neighbor's. It was hard to imagine Joe and Alicia having company that would arrive by limo. Someone had come to see Alex. A woman? God, why did that thought chill her so?

She hurried inside, expecting to hear laughter once again. Instead she heard a male voice, not Alex's, coming from the dining room. She hung her jacket on the coatrack and walked toward the voice. She didn't see Mimi in the living room, which was odd. And where was Chloe?

Her answer came as she entered the dining room. Mimi and Chloe were standing inside the kitchen, watching Alex and two strangers sitting at the table. She started to say hi, but Chloe put her finger to her lips. Dani walked slowly toward her daughter, trying to size up what was going on.

The two strangers were men. One, a nice-looking preppy kind of guy dressed casually in slacks and a long-sleeve white shirt, unbuttoned at the neck.

His thinning hair was blond and he wore wire-rimmed glasses. At the moment, he had a cellular phone in one hand, and a computer mouse in the other, and he was staring so intently at the laptop computer on the table that she didn't think he'd noticed her at all.

The other man was older, and dressed more conservatively in a very expensive-looking suit. His silver hair was thick, his skin tan and the lines that went from the edge of his nose to bracket his mouth were very deep. He, too, had a cellular phone, into which he was talking in a low growl. The older man did see her, although he dismissed her just as quickly.

Alex sat between them. He spoke to someone on yet another phone while he read from a stack of folders in front of him. His briefcase was on the table, open, and other papers covered the table from one end to the other.

She reached Chloe and Mimi. The older woman leaned close to whisper in her ear. "They got here a little before three. It's been like this all afternoon. Mr. Bradley hasn't been off the phone once. They've been calling all over the world. I sure hope they're not billing those calls to you. I don't even call Evelyn from here, and she's only in Colorado."

"Who are they?" Dani asked, also whispering, but wondering why it was necessary. It was her house, after all.

"That one's Ted," Chloe said, in her own attempt at being quiet, which didn't quite succeed. "He's a right-hand man. The other guy is a lawyer. From California. They flew in a private jet. Alex said I could fly in it if I wanted to. I want to. Can I?"

"We'll talk about that later," Dani said. "What about dinner?"

Mimi's hand flew to her mouth. "Oh, for mercy's sake, I forgot. Oh, heavens, I'm sorry. I'll start it right now."

Dani put a restraining hand on Mimi's shoulder. "Don't bother. We'll call out for pizza. I'm sure these gentlemen are hungry, too. I'll get a few." She walked over to her phone, but before she could lift the receiver, it rang. She jumped, then answered. "Hello."

"Alex Bradley, please," a very officious female voice said.

"Who's calling?"

"Mr. Trump."

Dani's mouth dropped open. "Donald Trump?"

"Yes, ma'am. Is Mr. Bradley available?"

Dani nodded, but realized the caller couldn't see her. "One moment, please." She put the receiver down and went to the dining room. Alex saw her then, and his smile was half warm and half apologetic. He was still speaking on his cellular.

"That call..." she said, not sure whether to interrupt or wait until he'd hung up.

"Hold on a sec," Alex said to his party. Then he looked up at her, waiting.

"It's Donald Trump," she said, trying hard not to sound as amazed as she felt.

"Tell him I'll call him back, would you? Find out where he is. Thanks, Dani. We'll be through here in a minute. I swear."

She nodded. As she walked back to the phone, she couldn't help wondering what the hell she was doing with a man who didn't have to take Donald Trump's phone calls. It seemed official now, fully signed, sealed and delivered that she was out of her league by a mile. While she was used to Tinkle the dachshund, he was talking to one of the richest men in the world. Wait, Alex was one of the richest men in the world. He should have his own Marla Maples, not a small town country vet like her.

She picked up the phone, and tried to sound like someone who knew what she was doing. "Mr. Bradley would like to know where he can return the call," she said.

Instead of the chewing out she expected, the woman just gave her the number, and told her that Mr. Trump would be there for the rest of the night, and he looked forward to the call.

Holy cow. Dani hung up the phone. So Mr. Trump didn't mind waiting for Alex. Although she knew there was nothing at all wrong with her, or her life, and that most people would be happy to have all she had, she suddenly felt quite like Little

Orphan Annie. No wonder Alex wanted her to be his mistress. He certainly couldn't take her out in public. What would his friends think? That he was slumming, no doubt.

Dully, she lifted the receiver once more, and hit the speed dial for Domino's. She ordered three large pizzas, wondering if her guests had ever even had pizza. Probably at Spago's. Made with goat cheese and caviar. Well, she couldn't do anything about that. They'd have to make do with pepperoni here.

She joined Chloe and Mimi, and watched the men at her table in silence. It was fascinating. The talk was fast and furious. The two men with Alex kept standing up and sitting down again. She couldn't keep up with the conversations, all simultaneous, one in French. But mostly she just stared at Alex.

Seeing him like this was a revelation. Of course she'd known he was a powerful man. She'd read the articles and seen the television shows. But seeing him in action made it all too real. Imagine, this man doing her laundry. She felt embarrassed to have ever entertained the idea. He was so far above that kind of thing it was laughable. But then she remembered him with Pete. Getting down on his hands and knees to crawl into the cage with his buddy. That's the Alex she had been attracted to. This Alex was, well, scary.

Only then did she realize he'd stopped talking.

Not just that. He was staring at her, even though
his young associate was talking to him. Alex didn't
pay attention, though. He stood, keeping his gaze
on her, and walked toward her. She heard the young
man say, "Alex!" in a very surprised and none too
happy tone. But still he kept coming.

He reached her the next moment. His smile almost made her forget who he was again. Almost.

"I'm sorry about this. I didn't know Ted was
going to come in person. I would have stopped him
if I had."

She swallowed, then mustered a smile. "It's
okay. Really."

"What about Chloe's dinner?"

"I've ordered some pizza. I hope they don't
mind."

His brow furrowed. "Who?"

"Your friends."

"Them? You don't have to feed them. Honest.
I'm going to chase them out anyway."

"Don't. Not on my account. I can see they need
you. It looks like it's important."

He shrugged. "The fate of the world doesn't
hang in the balance, Dani. It's just business."

"I'll bet."

"You don't believe me?"

"How can I when he keeps looking at me like
that."

Alex turned to see. His assistant was staring at
her, not too kindly. He seemed frustrated and anx-

ious, and she wondered how his blood pressure was.

Alex turned back. "Ignore Ted. Worry is his natural state. If he doesn't have a crisis once a day he goes into withdrawals."

"You should go back, anyway. I've got to change, and I want to go over Chloe's homework. It's not a problem."

"Sure? I can have them cleared out in five."

"No, thanks. But I appreciate the offer. You go. We'll talk when you're through."

He leaned down and kissed her lightly on the lips. It was enough to make her skin tingle, even though she knew his heart was only half engaged. Despite his reassurance, she could sense his impatience to get back to work. She had a premonition that a life with Alex would always include a battle between business and a personal life. One, she feared, where business would win hands down.

He left her with a smile, and she decided right then that she would go take a shower. She needed time to think. Seeing Alex in his world was as unsettling as it was confusing.

"Mimi, would you mind staying for a little bit longer?"

"Why?" Chloe asked. "Where are you going?"

"Nowhere. I'm just going to take a quick shower." She saw Mimi smile and nod, then turned back to Chloe. "Will you help her serve Alex and his friends some pizza?"

"Okay. Can I have soda?"

Dani nodded. "But only if you eat some salad, too."

Chloe made a face, but she didn't say no. Dani quickly found her purse and gave Mimi the money for the pizzas, and then she left the room. Alex's commanding voice was the last thing she heard before she closed the door to her bedroom.

As she undressed, she caught her image in the mirror. It stopped her. This was not the body of a supermodel. Or even a less than supermodel. While she was reasonably fit and trim, there was no mistaking that hers was a real woman's figure. Her breasts were beginning to lose their fight with gravity. Her stomach was a bit poochy and the stretch marks from having Chloe had faded, but not disappeared. She didn't even want to think about her butt. When she thought about the other women Alex had undoubtedly seen naked, she realized that there was no way, no how, that he was ever, ever going to see her without clothes.

How had she thought that this little fairy tale could have a happy ending? He was the prince, she was the frog, and no amount of kissing was going to transform her into his kind of princess.

At least her struggle was over. There were no more doubts, no more "what-ifs." Alex, with his charm and his looks and his sweet kisses, was going to leave her house and her life in two days. She wished it could be tonight. Getting over him was going to take a long time. She might as well start now.

Chapter Eleven

"We can have you back in New York tonight. There's a vet standing by to take care of Pete. I've got a driver here to take your car. Face it, Alex, you're letting the ball drop. People are starting to wonder."

Alex listened to Ted's words carefully. He knew his assistant was looking out for his welfare, and that it would be wise to do exactly as Ted suggested. "Sorry, Ted. No can do."

"What the hell does that mean?" Ted got up from the dining-room table and paced the small room. "Some charming colloquialism you picked up here in Hooterville?"

"Hey. Knock it off, Ted. It just means I'm not going. Not yet. I've made a commitment, and I'm going to honor it."

"What about your commitment to Trump? To Lysander and Colfax? What about the Toronto deal?"

"I can take care of all of that from here."

Ted shook his head. "What the hell's happened to you? Is it the woman?"

"Her name is Dani, and yes, since you asked so nicely, it is."

Ted stopped, then moved to the chair next to Alex's. "I don't mean any disrespect, but why? What's she got that you can't find in New York?"

"Oh, Ted. You really need some time off."

"Don't change the subject."

"Then stop being a jackass. I'm not talking about moving in here. It's just a few more days."

"Then what?"

"Then I'll come home. And if things go the way I want them to, Dani will come home with me."

"You want to marry her? You're kidding."

Alex cringed at Ted's shocked expression, and his words. But it wasn't anything he hadn't thought himself.

"What am I saying," Ted said, smiling cautiously. "You're smarter than that. You want to set her up in Manhattan? A nice penthouse for the mistress, close but not too close?"

Alex felt extremely uncomfortable discussing this with Ted, although he wasn't sure why. They'd always been open about his women before. But with Dani it was different. "We don't need to go into that now. Let's finish this business up, huh? Fallon isn't going to be happy you've made him wait so long in the car."

"Fallon is probably sound asleep. Besides, I'm

more concerned with you than him." Ted looked him squarely in the eye. "Tell me you won't do anything stupid. You've done nothing but preach the gospel of the right woman since the day I met you. Are you seriously going to screw that all up? A mistress is one thing, but the way you're talking..."

Alex pushed his chair back and stood up. He didn't want to discuss this anymore. Not with Ted. He just wanted his assistant out. "I'm not marrying anyone. I'm not screwing anything up. I just need a few days, that's all. So get going, huh?"

Ted shook his head, but he also started to put all his folders into his briefcase. Alex folded the empty pizza boxes and picked up the used napkins. By the time he walked Ted to the front door, it was eight-fifteen. He'd blown his dinner with Dani, and he wanted to find her to apologize. She'd said it didn't matter, but he didn't believe her.

Ted hesitated just as Alex was swinging the door shut. "All I ask," he said, "is that you think things through. Don't do anything rash."

"Thank you, Mother."

"You're welcome. I'll talk to you tomorrow."

Alex closed the door firmly, but he didn't move for a moment. He couldn't deny that Ted had shaken him up. Things had seemed much clearer this afternoon. But still, there was no way he was going to walk away from Dani. There had to be a workable solution that didn't throw both of their lives into chaos. Wasn't he supposed to be a master at problem-solving?

He might not be able to fix everything right now, but he sure could do some fence-mending when it came to Dani and their dinner plans. She was with Chloe now, and he headed toward the little girl's bedroom.

Chloe's door was open, and he saw Dani sitting on the edge of the twin bed. One soft light was on, and it bathed Dani in a hazy glow. He could only see her profile, and Chloe, tucked in with the covers up snugly against her chest. Dani was in a sweatshirt and jeans.

Chloe saw him and waved, using just her fingers. Dani turned at the movement, and smiled. He'd expected her to be upset, but she didn't appear to be.

"Come in," she said. "It seems Chloe has a question for you."

He walked into the little girl's room, curious. "A question for me?"

Dani nodded. "Yep. She won't tell me what it is, either."

"Hmm," Alex said, hoping like crazy the question was about NASDAQ prices or interest rates. Something he could answer.

"You have to sit on the bed," Chloe said. Then she turned to Dani. "And you can't listen."

Dani stood up and gave him a little shrug that told him she was to be held harmless. He nodded.

"I'm going to make some cocoa. You want some?"

"Sounds good. I'll meet you at the table."

She smiled at him, leaned down and kissed Chloe, then left the room. He wanted to join her, to tell her how sorry he was for changing their plans. Hell, he just wanted to look at her. Okay, so he wanted to kiss her. Maybe get in a touch or two. But first, there was Chloe.

Her room was just as unexpected as the girl herself. There were no dolls on shelves, no plush animal toys, except for one rather ratty looking stuffed pony sitting next to a computer on the desk. He did see a telescope, a microscope, a picture of Einstein and that picture of the Earth he liked so much. The one taken by the shuttle astronauts. Chloe certainly wasn't a typical eight-year-old.

"So what's this burning question?" he asked, hoping like hell it wasn't about physics.

"I heard you and Ted talking about my mom," she said. "And I was wondering. What's a mistress?"

On second thought, a physics question was just fine.

"Well?" Chloe prompted.

"Yes, well, let's see." He stood up. Walked away from the bed, casually, not running or anything, while he scrambled for an answer. The silence in the room was deafening. Weren't children supposed to be seen and not heard?

"A mistress is someone who runs her household," he said, praying he could get away with this interpretation. "It doesn't even have to be a household. It can be a business or even a group she's in charge of. Like, say, in England, they would call a landlady the mistress of the house. Or a school principal would be the headmistress."

"So you want Mommy to run your household?"

He blinked. Where were earthquakes when you needed them? "I've thought about that, yes. But we're just at the talking stage. I do like the idea of you and your mom coming to New York, though."

"Yeah, I do, too," Chloe said, lifting herself up on her elbows. "I've been looking up all this stuff on the internet about New York. It's so cool. They've got about a hundred museums, and there's this really huge park called Central Park where they have boats on the lake and you can skate there in the winter. And everything's open really, really late. And you can ride in carriages around the park, with real horses."

He sighed with relief. That had been a close one. Thank God Dani hadn't stuck around to hear. She'd have been plenty upset. He wasn't too thrilled himself. If he'd had a clue Chloe was anywhere near the dining room, he'd have kept his mouth shut, and Ted's, too.

He moved back over to Chloe's bed. "So you think you'd like it there, huh?"

She nodded enthusiastically. "Oh, yes. I'm not

very crazy about living here. But Mom has her clinic, and all the relatives and everything. She'd probably be sad to leave Grandma and Grandpa.''

"You wouldn't?"

She thought for a moment. "Yeah, I would. But we'd come back to visit. And they could come to visit us. Grandpa would love the lake with the boats. He really likes boats."

"Central Park is pretty neat. In the daytime, that is."

"So can we go?"

"That's up to your mother."

"Yes, it is."

Dani's voice made them both turn to look at the door. Alex had no idea how long she'd been standing there, or what she'd heard.

"Right now, it's time for someone to go to sleep."

"But, Mom. Alex knows all about New York. He can tell us everything."

"We'll talk about it another time, Chloe. Right now, it's lights out."

"Okay," she said, letting her head fall back on her pillow. "Only one more thing."

"What?" Dani asked, her voice full of suspicion.

Chloe turned to Alex. She crooked her finger for him to come closer. He leaned toward her.

"Closer," Chloe said.

He was already flush against the bed, so she must mean to lean down even more. He did.

"Closer."

He bent further. Now he was just inches from the little girl. She must want to whisper something in his ear. Something she didn't want Dani to know. He bent a last inch.

Chloe kissed him. On the cheek. Then she lay back down, turned to her side and closed her eyes.

It took Alex a while to get what had just happened. It was so unexpected, especially from Chloe. He liked it, though. More than he had any reason to. He bent down just that inch more and kissed her on her small soft cheek. "Sweet dreams, little one."

Then he straightened up, smiling, and after she turned off the light, he followed Dani.

She walked him down the hall until they were once again in the dining room. His computer was still open, and his files were stacked neatly next to it. "I'm sorry about tonight."

"It's all right. I know you're a busy man."

"I didn't ask them to come here."

"I know."

"And I never intended to miss our dinner."

"Please don't apologize. It's perfectly okay."

There was something in her tone he didn't like. A distance, a formality. Either she was angry, or worse, she'd changed her mind about him. That wouldn't do at all.

He walked toward her, determined to get his Dani back. To pick up where they'd left off at the clinic this afternoon. Damn Ted for showing up like that. Sure he'd needed to get his work done, but there was nothing that couldn't have waited, despite Ted's hysteria. Business was simply business. Dani was something else altogether.

Dani kept herself still. Even though she wanted to back away from Alex, she didn't. She had to be strong now, make her stand. She'd awakened tonight. Seen him clearly for the first time. Seen the different universe he occupied when he wasn't trapped in a one-horse town like Carlson's Gap.

The urge to run increased as he took the last few steps that brought him within touching distance. This wasn't going to be easy. He intoxicated her when he was this close. Her pulse speeded up, her heart pounded in her chest. She even felt her nipples harden, and she was grateful she'd put on this sweatshirt. She couldn't let him know how he affected her; it would give him too much ammunition.

"What's wrong, Dani?" He reached out and brushed the side of her cheek, gently.

Dani's eyes fluttered closed of their own volition. She struggled to gain her composure as she took hold of his hand and brought it down. "Nothing," she said, even though she knew he'd never accept the single statement.

"Please don't lock me out," he said. "Not now. Not when we're just getting started."

"There's nowhere to go, Alex. Nowhere but down."

His brows came together and the hurt in his face made her swallow hard. "What happened? Was it Ted? Did he say something to you?"

She shook her head. "No, he was perfectly nice. So was your attorney. But it was pretty clear that neither one of them understood why you haven't gone back." She took a step away from him. There was no choice. If she stayed too close she would buckle. "I think you should have gone back, too."

"Why? Just tell me."

"Because you're you. And I'm me."

"Now what in hell is that supposed to mean?"

"Don't get angry. I'm just trying to be honest here."

She saw him inhale deeply, then let the air out slowly. Why was the urge to comfort him so strong? It was utter foolishness to want to make him feel better just as she was trying to sever their tenuous bonds. It would have been much easier if she didn't like him so much. But that didn't matter. Not for what he had in mind.

"Honest? Are you going to tell me you don't feel anything toward me? Because I won't believe that. Not for a minute."

She shook her head. "No, I won't tell you that. If I didn't feel anything, maybe I'd really think about joining you in New York. The problem here is that I do. I like you, Alex. And I'm not ashamed to admit I'm attracted to you. But that's neither here nor there. The truth I'm talking about is that there's no hope for a future for us. Not the kind of future I want for myself. Or for Chloe.''

"If it's that mistress business—"

"Of course it's that mistress business. But it's more than that, too. Alex, you're Tiffany's. I'm Wal-Mart. It would never work.''

"You don't know that. How can you know that if you don't take a chance?''

"Because I'm a realist. And when you get back to your home turf, you'll be a realist, too. This is nuts. You're making too much of a physical attraction.''

"Dammit, Dani, it's not just that. You're not like anyone I've ever met before.''

"Exactly. I'm a small town hick, and for some reason that's caught your fancy. But what happens when you get bored with the shiny new toy? What happens to me, and to Chloe?''

He didn't say anything for a long minute. His face was serious, his brows still together in a disapproving V. He ran his hand through his hair, turned away from her, then turned back. All she wanted to do was run into his arms and tell him everything would be okay. She wanted his smile back, his quick wit, and mostly she wanted to see that look of longing in his eyes. But she believed what she was telling him. It couldn't end well. There was no chance of that. So best to get the hurt over and done with.

"What's impossible to fight," he said, his voice

so low she had to strain to hear him, "is this idea you have that I don't know what I'm doing. If you knew me better, you'd see that I'm not a romantic dope. I don't make decisions like these lightly."

"But I don't know you better."

"So the real enemy here is time, right?"

"That's only a part of it."

"What's the other part?"

"There's too big a gap between us," she said. She felt suddenly tired. More than tired. She pulled out a chair and sat down, knowing full well she couldn't have stayed on her feet for another moment. "I've lived here all my life. My family has lived here for four generations. I'm safe here, and so is my daughter. I'm not willing to give that up."

He took the chair next to hers and moved it over so he could face her closely, then he sat down. Reaching over gently, he captured her hand. His thumb rubbed her wrist softly, back and forth. "I don't want to steal you from your family and put you in some ivory tower. I've got a company jet that will be at your disposal, and there's no reason you and Chloe couldn't use it as often as you like."

She started to protest but he held up his free hand to stop her.

"The safety issue is a little trickier. New York can be a dangerous place, but there are ways to make yourself safer. I can help with that. I can't guarantee nothing bad would happen, but you can't guarantee that you wouldn't be hit by a milk truck tomorrow on Main Street. But I don't think that's the safety you're talking about.''

''No?'' she asked.

He shook his head. ''I think the reason you're so safe here is because you don't have to risk your heart. When's the last time you went out on a date?''

She took her hand out of his. ''I don't see what that has to do with anything. Even if it was your business.''

He leaned deliberately forward and retook her hand, holding it tightly so she couldn't break away. After a moment, she stopped trying to.

''Come on, Doc. Don't pull back now. Tell me. Was it this year? Last year? Have you been out with anyone since Chloe was born?''

She nodded. ''Yes, I have.''

''And?''

''It didn't work out.''

''It? One guy?''

''So I'm not promiscuous. Sue me.''

He laughed. God, that sound weakened her more than any of his logical questions or illogical assumptions. That, and his hand on hers. If she didn't make a clean getaway soon, she might crumble, and that would not be smart.

''Safety isn't all it's cracked up to be,'' he said. ''It's damn lonely. What's the worst thing that will happen if you come with me to New York?''

"I'll feel horribly out of place. Out of my league."

"I can safely promise that won't happen. You'll love New York. I know you will. Dani, it's a thrilling city, and it has so much to offer you. As for being out of your league, that's just plain not true. Despite the fact that I know a lot of wealthy people. They're not all jerks. Some of them are pretty decent. Almost as good as the folks right here in Carlson's Gap."

She studied his eyes, surprised at the fervor she saw there. "Why are you fighting so hard?" she asked. "That's what I don't understand. You don't know me well enough to want me like this."

He sat back with a jerk. She could see her question had startled him. But it had to be asked.

"I guess I am fighting pretty hard," he said. "But that's just who I am. When I know something is right, I don't let anything stand in my way."

"And you know I'm something right?"

He nodded. "Beyond a shadow of a doubt."

"I wish I could be so sure."

"I think you already are. It's the fear that's stopping you, Dani. Trust me, you won't feel lost or alone. I won't let that happen."

"There are some things even you can't protect me from," she said, pulling her hand free once more. She stood up before he could grab it again. "You can't protect me from a broken heart."

"I'd never hurt you, honey. Never."

"Don't say that. You know it's not true."

He stood, too, but he didn't try to touch her again. He simply captured her gaze and held it steady with an intensity that kept her from moving an inch. "You can stay here," he said, "and be safe and secure and watch your daughter grow up, and your practice flourish. You might even meet some nice guy, and decide to get married. But you'll always know that you had a chance for magic, and you let it pass you by."

"Magic?"

He nodded. Then he lifted his hand and brought it slowly toward her. He touched her arm with the tips of his fingers, and she jumped from the spark. She didn't see it with her eyes, but she felt the shock course through her. Up and down her arms, through her chest, down her legs, settling at the juncture of her thighs. Just from a touch. Just from his touch.

"Magic."

Chapter Twelve

"What's all this?" Dani stood in the laundry room, amazed and mystified by the stacks of neatly folded clothes on the low utility table. Everything was clean. Blouses, slacks and skirts were hung on the rack, towels and sheets were separated by color.

"Hmm," Alex said, moving up behind her...close behind her. He put his hand on her waist, tentatively at first, then firmed his grip and pulled her back so she was flush against him. "Looks like the laundry fairy paid you a visit."

"But you were sleeping. I saw—"

Alex turned her around. "You saw me? And when was that, you little voyeur?"

She felt her cheeks flush. Not just because she'd let it slip that she'd peeked in on him during the night, but because he held her so close to him that she felt her body get all moist and tingly. The magic was back, full force. As much as she'd like to deny that, she couldn't. She betrayed herself every time she touched him. "I looked in on you, yes," she said, trying hard to keep her voice steady and guard her eyes so he wouldn't see what he was doing to her. "Just to make sure everything was okay."

"Was it?"

"Yes. You were sleeping very soundly. I thought for the night."

He nodded. "I did sleep through the night. I told you. It was the laundry fairy."

"Alex, of all the things I could call you, a fairy isn't one of them."

He grinned. It was impossible not to grin back. Lord, how handsome he was. In his simple white shirt, sleeves rolled up revealing the muscled forearms with a smattering of dark hair that made him all the more masculine, and his jeans, just tight enough to show off his award-winning butt, he was devastating. But just because he turned her to mush, she wasn't going to take back what she'd said last night.

"There's only one thing I want you to call me, Doc."

"What's that?"

"Lover." Then he leaned forward, her eyes fluttered closed and then his mouth took hers captive.

He didn't use force. He used skill. His lips touched hers lightly at first, then the pressure increased until she knew she was being soundly, stunningly kissed. When he let up, she opened her mouth to protest, which must have been what he'd counted on, for in that second, he snuck his tongue inside her mouth and tasted her, awakening sensations that had no business being awake.

Using his hands on her back, massaging, exploring, squeezing her flesh oh so gently, he outmaneuvered her on both flanks. She pulled back for a second, realized it was hopeless and sent up the white flag. She kissed him back.

Alex knew the moment she let go. The moment she shed her inhibitions and responded like no other woman alive. Her taste, slightly sweet and slightly coffee, was as intoxicating as champagne. Her scent, a mixture of pure woman and summer flowers, snaked inside him and turned him into a cauldron of need. Her feel, soft, feminine, curvy and delicate, made him swell painfully against his jeans. And when she nibbled on his lower lip, teased him with her tongue, ran her hand down his back, he wanted to take her right there. On the dryer. On the table. Against the wall. It didn't matter, as long as he could take possession of the one thing he wanted more than anything else in the world. Dani. His Dani.

No longer thinking with reason, he moved his right hand to her breast and the second he touched her rigid nipple beneath her blouse, he groaned and pressed against her lower belly. He heard her moan in response, and that was it. He couldn't take any more. Moving her back toward the low table, he grabbed her thighs just below her derrière, and lifted her onto the table. He spread her knees apart and moved into that space, never letting go of her lips, never letting the contact between them widen.

She pulled back for a second and whispered, "Chloe."

Without missing a beat, he stuck his leg out, caught the edge of the door and shoved it closed.

"Oh, my," she said, and he inhaled the words as he brought his mouth down on hers once more.

He felt her arms come around his neck, and the insanely sensuous feel of her fingers in his hair. As his head swam and his body boiled, he used his fingers to unbutton her blouse. Quickly, carefully, and then he was touching the soft skin of the top of her breast and the silky bra that held her for him. His thumbs traced the outline of the bra, then slipped underneath, just for a second.

He pulled back from their kiss and looked at her. She took his breath away with her beauty. This is how he always wanted her. Hungry. Needing him. Mouth parted slightly. Tinge of pink on her cheeks. Eyes half closed and filled with desire. No mortal man could fail to be moved, and God knows, he was only flesh and blood.

Although he never wanted to stop looking at her, there was more to do. So much more. He leaned down, drinking in the sight of her breasts. Her nipples, as hard as erasers, pushed the silky pink fabric invitingly, and he lowered his lips first to her right bud. Circling the hard nub with his tongue, feeling it swell even further, he took the hidden flesh in his teeth, very gently, then sucked in sharply.

Her gasp was his reward. No longer content to toy with her, he unclasped the front opening of the bra and peeled it back, letting go with his mouth at the last possible second. She was completely exquisite. Her breasts, pale and high and firm, showed her arousal so clearly it made him crazy. He cupped her right breast in his hand while he gave her left nipple his mouth's attention. Tasting her skin was too much. Feeling her arch her back was more than he could stand. And when he felt her hand on his jeans, and then, merciful heaven, on his erection, he nearly came right then.

"Oh, Alex," she murmured as she felt his heat. "I want…"

He found her hand and pressed it to him more firmly, echoing her words with his body.

"Dani," he whispered, not leaving her breast. Then words were impossible with his tongue and his lips so busy.

"Mom! I'm gonna be late again!"

He felt Dani freeze. Her hand pulled away. The arch in her back straightened, and he groaned in frustration.

"Chloe," Dani said urgently.

What could he do? He backed away, unable to look at her. If he did, he'd never let her go, Chloe or no Chloe.

"I'm sorry," she said. Out of the corner of his

eye he saw her struggle with her bra and then her blouse. He was struggling with something much more personal.

"I think Pete can come home today. If you want, you can come to the clinic this afternoon to get him, or I can just bring him home."

He nodded, knowing that wasn't an answer, but unable to speak.

"I'll call you later."

He heard her jump down from the table. "Or you can call me."

She moved to the door.

"Oh, damn," she said.

Then the door opened and closed. He leaned hard against the cold wall. It didn't help. He had a terrible feeling nothing would.

SOMEHOW, DANI MANAGED to get through the day. Five dogs, seven cats, two parakeets and one gerbil took her mind off Alex intermittently, although nothing had taken him completely away. It was as if his touch had come with her to work. She could still feel every spot on her body that he'd caressed. She had never been more grateful for the white lab coat she wore, as her nipples had remained hard all day. She hadn't known they could do that. Of course, she had to wonder if Alex had stayed that way, too. For his sake, she hoped not. Although the idea of doing that to him did appeal to some very primitive, very naughty part of her.

He'd phoned her at ten. She'd called him at noon. Then again at two. Since she was bringing Pete home with her, he hadn't come to visit, which was for the best. If she was having this much trouble with him so many blocks away, everything would have fallen apart if she'd actually seen him.

But now that her last patient was gone, she couldn't hurry enough. Pete was really doing well, and he was almost as anxious as she was to get home to Alex. His whole body quivered as she locked up the clinic, and never had she identified more with her canine friends. Her own quivering wasn't quite so obvious, but it was there, all right.

Knowing it was all wrong, that a relationship with Alex would never work, hadn't made a bit of difference. Her logic and her body were at odds with each other, and right now logic wasn't winning. All she could think of was getting home. Seeing his smile. Hearing his voice. Feeling his touch.

Finally she opened her front door. The first thing she noticed was that Mimi wasn't in the living room, and the TV was off. She led Pete toward the kitchen and he must have gotten Alex's scent because halfway there, he started leading her. They'd just hit the kitchen door when they both saw Alex.

He stood at the stove, stirring something hot in a big pot. He put down the spoon, turned, and with a smile that was pure little boy, said, ''Welcome home.''

He kept his gaze on her as he squatted down for

Pete. The old dog bounded across the floor, and nearly knocked him over. But still, Alex looked at her. Until, that is, Pete started licking his face.

"Mom, guess what? Who's that?"

Chloe stood beside her, staring at Alex and Pete. She still had on her school clothes—a green jumper with a turtleneck underneath—but she was also sporting a red baseball cap with the brim turned around. Dani was a little startled to see that her daughter had sprouted again. She came up to the middle of her upper arm, where just a few weeks ago, she'd reached her elbow. She was growing up so quickly.

She leaned over and kissed her little girl on the cheek. "That's Pete," she said. "Alex's dog."

"Cool. Can I pet him?"

"Sure. But I'd wait for the homecoming to be over first."

Chloe nodded.

"What were you going to tell me?" Dani asked.

"Oh, yeah. Guess what?"

"What?"

"We have to make two cakes. It's for the school booth. One's supposed to be chocolate and the other is supposed to be something else."

"We? You got a mouse in your pocket?"

"It's supposed to be a mother-daughter project. And I've never baked a cake before."

Dani narrowed her eyes. "When do we have to bake these cakes?"

"Tonight."

"Uh-huh. And when did you find out about this project?"

Chloe blushed. "Two weeks ago."

"And you didn't tell me then because…?"

"I forgot. Oh, and we're not supposed to use a mix. And I have to bring the recipes to school on three-by-five cards so they can be in the cookbook."

Dani sighed. "No mix?"

Chloe shook her head. "Mr. Tompkins said that we should find out if there are any old family recipes, like from our grandparents. We're supposed to write something about that."

"Good idea," Dani said. "I'm sure Grandma would love to help you with the cakes."

"I can help."

Dani and Chloe both blinked, then turned to Alex. He'd risen, although his hand was still busy petting Pete's head.

"You?" Dani asked. She tried really hard not to laugh out loud. She couldn't do much about her grin, though.

"Hey, who do you think cooked dinner?"

She looked at her kitchen. In addition to the pot on the stove, there were several other pots and pans in or near the sink. Her old punch bowl, which was given to her by her aunt Esther, but which she'd never used, appeared to be filled with lettuce and tomatoes. There was also an assortment of spice jars, oil, vinegar, salt, flour, baking soda and some other unidentifiable food containers lined up on the counter. "My goodness," she said. "Bored, were we?"

Alex approached her, Pete tagging along, obviously happy to be with his master again. "I wasn't bored at all. This cooking thing is interesting. Easier than I thought it would be."

"Oh?" She let him lead her to the stove. He took the lid off the pot, and she smelled chicken and garlic. Lots of garlic. "What's this?"

"It's soup. But that's not the main course. That's in the oven."

She pulled down the door to the oven and saw a whole bird roasting inside. From here, it looked good. Brown-skinned, juicy. Next to it was a covered casserole. "And?"

"Stuffing."

She closed the door. "I didn't know I had everything to make such a sumptuous meal. Thank you. May I ask what brought on this mad rush of domesticity?"

"I promised you a good dinner. I didn't want to leave Pete his first night home, so the next best thing was to do it myself."

She crossed her arms and looked at him, standing there so proudly you'd have thought he'd just invented chicken itself.

"The only thing we don't have is dessert."

"We're not big on desserts here—"

"We can make the cakes!" Chloe said, blithely interrupting. "We can make three, and eat one tonight."

"Sure we can," Alex said, before Dani had a chance to catch her breath. "It'll be fun. The three of us can each work on one."

"Cool!" Chloe turned to her, her eyes already pleading, and her feet doing her little begging jig. "Please, Mom. Can we? Alex said he wants to. I want to. It'll be fun. I want to do the chocolate. With lots of icing. And three layers, okay?"

"Hold on. First, I don't have the ingredients for three cakes just lying around. I don't even have cake pans."

"We can get them. Okay?"

She looked from Alex to Chloe and back again. How was she supposed to say anything but yes to those two faces? It would be like kicking a couple of puppies. "All right."

Chloe jumped up, straight in the air. Alex looked as if he wanted to join her. All Dani could do was shake her head. Which reminded her... "Where's Mimi?"

"I gave her the day off," Alex said. "I was here. So she didn't have to be."

"I see." She looked at Chloe suspiciously. "And what did we have for our afternoon snack?"

Chloe wasn't jumping anymore. She turned her guilty gaze away. "Just some cookies."

"Cookies? No wonder you're hopping all over

the place. And you want cake, too? Honey, you'll never sleep a wink tonight.''

"I will, too. I swear." She crossed her heart with her finger. "Honest."

Alex was looking a little guilty, too. "What was she supposed to have?"

"Fruit. Or half a sandwich. Or some cereal."

"Ah-hah," he said. "Got it." He scowled at Chloe. "As for you, little sneak." He crouched down and headed for her, mischief in his eyes and his hands poised for tickling. Chloe backed up, her giggles filling the kitchen. Pete got into the act with two spirited barks.

All in all, Dani couldn't remember a happier time. Just hearing Chloe sound like a little girl was enough to send her spinning, but watching Alex capture her in his arms, swing her into the air, laugh with her, tickle her and finally hold Chloe close, like a father would hold a daughter, was nearly too much to bear.

She turned to the stove, not anxious for either one of them to see her sudden tears. Why she felt so choked up was easy to explain. It was Chloe. She hardly ever laughed that way anymore. It wasn't necessarily because Alex was the one that incited that laughter, or that they looked so happy together. A stranger might think they were father and daughter. Damn.

With the back of her hand, she wiped the two tears that escaped, then lifted the pot cover. It took her a moment to focus, though, and she stirred the soup until she felt in control.

"Tell you what," Alex said. "Why don't we make those cakes, but we'll save them for tomorrow, huh?"

"Ahhhhh," Chloe whined. "That's no fun."

"Guaranteed dessert for several days to come is no fun?" Then Dani heard him whisper, "Someone's going to have to lick the spoons, remember. I think that's mandatory. I think I read about that in Betty Crockett."

Chloe giggled again. "Betty *Crocker.*"

"Ah. I wondered why there were no bear recipes in that book."

Dani laughed. Chloe said, "Huh?" Alex sighed and said, "Never mind."

Composed once more, Dani faced the two of them. To her surprise, Alex hadn't let Chloe go, and her daughter showed no signs of wanting to leave. He was leaning against the fridge. His arms were crisscrossed over Chloe's chest. Chloe was holding on to him, just above his elbows. Dani had never wanted to kiss Alex so badly. Or hug her baby so much.

She caught Alex looking at her, though. He crooked his head a bit, asking her what was wrong in that silent way that he had. She just smiled. She wasn't going to tell him what she was feeling, though. It would be too hard to extricate herself. The ammunition would be too great.

"So what time is this feast supposed to be ready?"

"Any minute," Alex said. "Just enough time for me to give Pete some food and water." He bent over Chloe's head to look at her upside-down. "You gonna help?"

"Yes!" she said. With that, she was off like a rocket. And he wanted her to lick the spoons.

"Come on, Pete. We've got dog food in the garage."

Pete looked at Alex, and only when his master nodded did the dog take off after Chloe. My God, it was like something out of Lassie. Next thing you know, Pete would be telling them that Timmy had fallen in the well.

"You want some wine?" Alex asked.

She shook her head. "Not if there's going to be baking later."

He moved toward her slowly. His demeanor had changed, and she was pretty clear about what he intended to do. If she had a brain in her head, she'd clear out. Go take a quick shower. At least wash her face. Instead she just stood there, waiting. No. Anticipating. She wanted his kiss. Oh, God, did she ever.

Unfortunately, Chloe and Pete made a reappearance that threw that idea out the window. Grabbing a rare flash of sanity, she fled, knowing she was just putting off the inevitable. But she had to regroup if she wanted to get out of this one. The question was, did she want to?

ALEX SET THE TABLE by himself. He poured the water all around, milk for Chloe and sparkling water for grown-ups. He set out salad plates, and a separate cruet of homemade dressing. He brought the bird to the two lovely ladies, and placed it on the hot pad with all the flair he could muster. He tried to imagine what would have happened if Ted had decided to show up tonight instead of last night. The poor guy probably would have had a coronary. He'd never have believed that Alex had fixed this perfect meal all by himself.

"It looks wonderful," Dani said.

Music to his ears.

"Smells good, too," Chloe added.

He just smiled. "Wait till you taste it." He ladled some soup into Chloe's bowl, then Dani's and finally his own. Then it was his turn to sit. He did, and then something strange hit him. A thought. No, more like déjà vu, only he'd never experienced this before. Well, not for real. This was a remembrance of a dream. Of a picture-perfect family he'd only imagined. A sense of belonging so strong it made his chest hurt. This family. *His* family.

Only it wasn't. At least, not yet.

Chapter Thirteen

Dani couldn't get over the beautifully set table. It really looked great, and the fact that Alex had gone to so much trouble wasn't lost on her at all. He was trying so hard to impress her. To show her that he was thinking of her. The problem was, it was working.

No man in her life had ever put so much effort, so much thought into pleasing her. She didn't like to admit it, but it had occurred to her more than once that if he was this attentive outside of the bedroom, she couldn't even imagine what he would be like between the sheets. If he continued to charm her this way, she had a sneaking suspicion she might find out.

She lifted her soupspoon, curious to test his culinary skills. It smelled good, although a little garlicky. Well, a little garlic never hurt anyone. He was watching her, so she figured whatever it tasted like, she was going to say something complimentary.

Hopefully Chloe would remember some of their past etiquette talks, and do the same.

She brought the soup to her lips, and swallowed. At first, she just noticed hot. Then she was on fire! Struggling not to cough or choke, her mouth blazing, she grabbed her water but then she saw Chloe bringing her own spoon to her lips, and she put down her glass, stood up in her chair, lunged for the spoon and yelled, "Stop!"

Chloe did. She froze, looking at Dani as if she'd lost her mind. Dani couldn't explain. She couldn't talk yet. She just got her glass once more and this time, she chugged the cold water. Her eyes were tearing and her cheeks were warm and all she wanted was for the fire in her mouth to stop. My God, what had he put in the soup?

She turned to look at him. Alex had the same stunned expression on his face as Chloe. He hadn't tasted the soup yet, either, thank goodness.

She finished the water, then took Chloe's glass of milk and drank that. Finally she could speak again. Calmly she sat back in her chair, and tried to smile at Alex.

The corner of his mouth quirked up. "That good, eh?"

She felt her cheeks get warmer still. "Um, it's a little…spicy."

"Yeah?" He brought the spoon up and tasted the soup, but just a tiny bit with the tip of his tongue. Dani waited. Two seconds later, she saw him swallow, hard. He sort of gasped, then got his water and downed the drink. When he finished, he put the glass down slowly, then turned back to face her. "Oops."

"What did you put in there?"

He shrugged. "Just what the recipe called for. Except for the pepper."

"The pepper?"

"You were out of black pepper, so I used red."

"Did the bottle say Cayenne?"

He nodded.

"How much?"

"A couple of tablespoons, I think."

She nodded. That would explain it. "Ah. Tablespoons. I think that's the problem. Cayenne pepper can go a long way."

"So I see."

She felt just terrible for him. If there'd been any way to eat the soup, she would have done it in a heartbeat. But as it was, they would have had to call the fire department to revive her if she tried. "Let's start on the chicken. That smells wonderful."

Alex's happy confidence was clearly shaken. He frowned as he went to the bird and started carving. After a couple of slices, he paused. "Maybe I should try this one, first, huh?"

Dani held out her plate. "Don't be silly. It looks perfect."

"You're sure?"

She nodded. He gave her the chicken, then scooped up some stuffing and doled out some green beans. Dani took her full plate and smiled. "Fit for a queen," she said.

"Uh-huh," Alex said as he fixed a meal for Chloe.

"Did you use cayenne on the chicken?" Dani asked.

"Nope."

He handed Chloe her plate, then fixed his own. He sat, watching Dani as she prepared to taste the food. Actually both of them watched her. She cut a small piece, brought it to her mouth and ate it.

He'd been right. No fires started. She could taste the chicken, but only slightly. What she really tasted was garlic. Lots and lots and lots of garlic. She smiled as she chewed, and then swallowed. "Mmm," she said, trying really hard to sound sincere. "This is great, Alex."

His eyes narrowed. "Why don't I believe you?"

"No, really. I like garlic."

He stared down at his own plate, then took a bite. He chewed slowly, the doubt on his face turning to a grimace. "You like this?" he asked.

"Sure," she said. "It's...different."

"It's awful."

"The stuffing is good," Chloe said.

Just then, the doorbell rang. As Dani got up, Alex turned to Chloe. "It's okay, kiddo. You don't have to lie. We'll go out and get something else for dinner.''

Chloe put her fork down a little too quickly. Dani's heart sank. She'd wanted this meal to be perfect. The doorbell rang again, and she went to answer it. Two of the women from the weekend steering committee stood before her. Their cheerful smiles faded when they saw her instead of Alex.

''Hi, hon,'' Brenda Holt said. The woman was a casual acquaintance, someone she knew from Chloe's school. Although Dani had never seen her dressed quite like this before. The black dress she wore had clearly been painted on. Not to mention her makeup.

''Is he here?'' Katie Elders whispered, leaning in conspiratorially. She was another woman from the school, but Dani knew her better than Brenda. Katie was normally a very sensible woman. They'd often met for lunch, or at the park. Only the great Alex disease had stricken her, too, it seemed, as she was wearing a pair of skintight jeans and a very snug sweater. Not her usual attire at all.

''We're having dinner,'' Dani said, wanting them both to leave now. Her ire surprised her. It was stronger than ever, too strong for the situation, really. The thought that it might actually be jealousy came and fled quickly. She couldn't be jealous. She wasn't the type.

''We just need him for a few minutes,'' Brenda

said. "Honest. We just need to go over some of the details about tomorrow."

"But…"

"Don't mind about dinner," Katie interrupted. "It won't bother us."

With that, the women entered. They didn't exactly bowl her over, or push her aside, but it was damn close. She doubted they heard her close the door as they walked quickly toward the dining room. Dani hurried after them, determined to get them out ASAP.

Alex was just standing as she rounded the corner. His smile was gracious, but cool. That made her feel a bit better.

"Mr. Bradley?" Brenda said breathlessly. "I'm the head of the steering committee for tomorrow's festivities. Brenda Holt."

"I'm Katie. I'm on the committee, too."

"We won't take but a minute of your time," Brenda said, moving a little bit in front of Katie. "So please, go on with your dinner. We just wanted to give you the details about your appearance."

Katie wasn't happy with her position, and stepped a little closer to the man of the hour, half blocking Brenda. Brenda didn't seem to like that, and she stepped in front of Katie. Dani figured at this rate, there would be bloodshed in a few minutes. Time for an intervention. She wanted these two out of here, but that didn't seem likely without a court order. Then she got an idea. A doozy.

"Well, we were just sitting down," she said. "You know, Alex fixed this meal himself."

"Oh!" Katie said.

"Really!" Brenda echoed.

"Yes. Maybe you'd like to join us? I can start you out with a little soup."

"But, Mom," Chloe said. Dani quickly put her hand on her daughter's shoulder and squeezed.

"I know you're not hungry, honey," she said, as if butter wouldn't melt in her mouth. "So you can be excused."

"But..."

"Go on, now."

Chloe got up slowly, looked at her with a very grown-up frown and left. Dani didn't dare look at Alex.

In the meantime, Katie and Brenda had found seats. Near Alex, of course. They both sat so straight in their chairs, were so atwitter at dining on Alex's meal, that she could barely contain her laughter. "I'll be right back with the first course."

She hurried into the kitchen. Brenda started telling Alex what time and where they had to be in the afternoon. Katie tried to get a word in edgewise, but that wasn't very successful. Dani got down two bowls, knowing she was going to hell for this little dirty deed, but not caring a whole heck of a lot. Then she heard Alex excuse himself.

He came up behind her just as she was ladling

the first bowl. His hand touched her shoulder. "What are you doing?"

She realized then that she couldn't go through with it, and put the bowl and spoon down. "Okay. I won't. But you'd think they'd have enough sense not to barge in on someone's dinner."

"I don't think they meant any harm."

"No? Then why are they dressed like the harlot sisters?"

Alex studied her for a moment. His eyes widened and his mouth quirked up. "Could it be? Are you…"

"No," she said. She darted past him, and hurried back to the dining room. "I'm sorry. The soup is gone already. We do have some salad, though, if you'd like."

Brenda looked to Katie, then back to Dani. "Did he make this chicken?" she asked.

"Yes," Dani said, "but…"

"I'd love to try some. If you don't mind."

Dani felt Alex come up behind her. Not just behind her but touching. The spark hit her, as always, the minute he made contact. It was just his shoulder against her back, but it was enough.

"It's not very good," Alex said. "I don't think you'd care for it."

"No, no," Brenda said. "It smells heavenly." She reached for a slice that was still on the carving platter, taking the small piece delicately between two fingers. Smiling broadly, she popped it into her mouth. Dani was quite impressed with her acting ability. She actually looked as if she was enjoying the taste.

Not to be outdone, Katie also helped herself. She managed to say, "Mmm."

The sight of the two of them, chewing, smiling, trying so hard, was something to see. Although she shouldn't, it was wrong, terribly wrong, Dani grinned. And grinned harder when she felt Alex's gentle pinch on her behind.

"You ladies don't have to be polite on my account," Alex said, walking around Dani back to his seat. "It seems I messed up on the garlic."

"No, not at all," Katie said. "It's delicious."

"Would you like some more?" Dani asked.

"No, no. Thanks," Katie said, her cheeks infusing with pink. "I've had dinner already."

"Me, too," Brenda said.

"What else can we do for you, then?" Dani asked, moving toward the hallway, trying to give them a hint.

The women looked at each other, then looked at Alex. Katie's shoulders sagged a bit. That did it. Now Dani really did feel guilty. These were nice women. They hadn't come here trying to steal Alex away. Well, maybe they had, but it was only natural. He was the Sexiest Man in the World, after all.

She looked at him, sitting so casually at her table, with his horrible meal spread out before him. It hit her that the sobriquet wasn't just a piece of marketing copy to her anymore. He was the sexiest man in the world. In her world, at least.

And she wanted him.

His gaze met hers just then. Just at that second when her head, her heart and her libido all came together with an almost audible clunk. The seconds stretched out as he stared at her. Somehow, he'd read her thoughts. She could see it plainly. He knew what she was thinking and his own gaze picked up her hunger. The same want was reflected in his eyes. It was telepathy. Magic.

"We'll see you two tomorrow then."

Dani was jerked back to reality. She had forgotten the women, forgotten the rest of the world for a moment there. It was hard to get her bearings, but she did. Then Alex got up and joined her, and together they walked Brenda and Katie to the door.

She wanted to reach out and take his hand. The urge to touch him was a physical thing.

Alex thanked the two women, and tried to be patient as he promised to be at the mall at exactly one o'clock tomorrow. He was even able to smile, to be polite. Dani said goodbye to them, too, but she sounded as distracted as he felt.

The second the door was closed, he took her in his arms and crushed her lips with the kiss that had begun in the dining room. The kiss she'd promised with her eyes.

Her arms went around his neck and she pulled

him tighter, the desperation in her gesture as acute as his own. Something had happened to her back there, some switch had gone from Off to On, and he'd seen it immediately. He had no idea what it was. Didn't care, really. Just so long as she was in his arms.

"Mom?"

He groaned, and felt her moan with his lips. Neither pulled away, though. He just couldn't let go of her. Not yet.

"Can you guys stop kissing for one second and tell me what I'm supposed to do about dinner?"

Dani pulled back, and he let her go. Well, not all the way. He wrapped his arm around her waist and kept her back pressed to him.

"I'll call out for a pizza," Dani said.

"We had pizza last night." Chloe stood in the hallway with her arms crossed over her chest. He was amazed at the resemblance between mother and daughter. She was a little Dani, right down to the shape of her nose. He could see there was a little influence from her father. Her height, for one thing. And something about her eyes. But she would end up beautiful, just like her mom. Lucky girl.

"Then how about a frozen burrito?"

"I want pancakes."

"For dinner?"

Chloe nodded. "Like Mimi makes them."

Dani turned her head quickly, shooting a glance at Alex. She was trying to tell him something, but he wasn't quite sure what. But she sure seemed excited about it.

"Wait one second," she said, and extricated herself from his hold.

Alex watched her hurry to the phone. He couldn't hear the conversation, and his curiosity was piqued. Something told him he was going to like this plan, whatever it was. Dani's smile when she hung up confirmed it.

"You," she said to Chloe, "can go pack a bag for the night."

"I can?" Chloe looked at her mom suspiciously. "Why?"

"Because you're going to get your pancakes. Just like Mimi makes them. At Mimi's house. You're going to have a sleepover."

Chloe grinned. "Cool." Then the worried look came back. "But what about the cakes?"

Dani's smile weakened. "Oh. I forgot."

"Hey," Alex said, knowing he was throwing away a golden opportunity. "I did promise to help."

No one responded. He caught the look that passed between Dani and Chloe, however. He grinned. "I promise. I'll let you guys check every ingredient before I put it in. No cayenne. No garlic."

Chloe giggled. Dani met his gaze. "You sure?" she whispered.

He nodded. Her smile was almost all the reward he needed. The real prize would come later.

DANI FINISHED WIPING the counter and put the sponge down. Dinner, which had turned out to be macaroni and cheese by default, had been eaten. Cakes had been baked, even though two quick trips to the store had been required. Icing had been licked. Now Chloe was in bed, Pete was sleeping soundly on a soft blanket in the living room, the kitchen was clean and she was alone with Alex.

She felt like a teenager on her first date. No, worse. A lovesick teenager faced with her biggest crush. Her skin felt tight, her breathing rapid. Her hand kept going to her hair, her gaze darting back and forth from his eyes to the floor. She laughed, and it sounded foolish and jittery. Something had to give soon, or she was going to lose it altogether and…

And what? The short answer was run like hell. The long answer was too complicated for her over-extended brain to consider.

Then the problem was whisked away. He took two steps, that's all, just two. He held out his arms. She entered his embrace. And everything that had happened in her world before that moment was gone. Just gone.

Suddenly she was being carried, cradled in his arms even while they kissed. Passion flowed between them as if it were an electrical current, held them together through the interminable walk to her bedroom. Once inside, with the door shut, he walked right to the bed and carried her with him on top of it, so they were laying next to each other, entwined with each other. His hands moved over her back in a frenzy of exploration, while she moved her hips and her thighs and her chest so that she could feel him in every possible way.

He moaned as her tummy rubbed his erection, and cupped her behind to pull her closer. The feeling of that hardness against her was almost more than she could take. She had never felt this kind of animal lust before. This desperation to have a man inside her. This man. Whose kisses turned her to mush. Whose caress made her melt. Who had far too many clothes on.

She reached for his shirt buttons and found her fingers so shaky it was difficult to maneuver. Alex helped, but as he reached the button just above his belt he stopped.

Dani looked at him, questioning.

"Are you sure?" he asked.

"Yes. Are you?"

She expected a quick yes in return. Instead he grew silent and still. "What's wrong?"

"Once will never be enough," he said.

Her hand went to his bare chest and she ran her fingers through the dark, soft, curly hair that covered his muscled flesh. "Who said anything about once?"

"I don't mean tonight," he said. "I mean that once I have you, I'll never let you go."

Oh, Lord, how she wanted to believe him. But it was enough to know that he was sincere. For tonight, he really did mean it. That his sentiments would change once he was back in the real world was a certainty, but right now, in this magic space, she decided not to think about that.

Her decision had been made hours ago, she realized. The moment she'd seen Alex standing in the kitchen, stirring his horrible soup. It hadn't been a hard decision after all. She would lose him no matter what. Whether they made love or not. But did she also want to regret passing up what could be the most intensely satisfying and beautiful night of her life? No. She'd lived on bittersweet memories for years. But tonight, and forever more, she would know that once she had been loved by the most wonderful man in the world.

She kissed him her answer, showed him her response with her hands and her body.

He cupped her face and looked deeply into her eyes. "I love you," he said.

She swallowed the lump in her throat, and whispered, "I love you, too."

Then his hand went to her breast, and she abandoned herself to the dream.

Chapter Fourteen

Her body. Petite, feminine, soft, so soft. Her blouse was off now, tossed to the floor, and his fingers were at the clasp of her pink bra. Even though the only light in the room came from a small lamp on her dresser, he could see how aroused she was. The nipples he'd touched so briefly this morning had remained in his memory all day. Truth be known, it was probably those very nipples that had made him screw up dinner. He laughed a little at the thought.

"What?" Dani asked softly.

"Nothing," he said. "Lord, you're so beautiful." He undid her bra, but he didn't expose her breasts yet. Instead he leaned down and ran his tongue between them, tasting the bare skin, breathing deeply to memorize her scent.

She sighed and pushed her chest a tiny bit toward him. As he continued to lick her, he carefully brought his fingers underneath the cups of her bra and teased the very edge of her sensitive flesh.

Dani moved beneath him, responsive, sensual. He had to fight the urge to rush. This was their first time, and there would be no hurrying. He wanted to savor every moment, every touch, every sound.

He moved his fingers up a bit more, so that the tips rested just beneath her areolae. The swell of her breasts filled the palms of his hands. She pushed again, urging him on. He took the right edge of her bra clasp in his teeth, then lifted the material slowly, slowly back and away, as if he were unwrapping a most precious present. The gift inside was her straining nipple, pink, erect and perfect. Now he leaned down again and this time he tasted the little bud with the tip of his tongue, then captured it gently between his teeth.

"Oh, Alex," she said as she writhed beneath him. Her hands went to the back of his head, and she grabbed his hair as if she needed to hang on to something before she fell. He used his hands to slide her pants down, but he didn't stop his ministrations. He couldn't have stopped for anything. Not even the end of the world.

He loved the taste of her. Nibbling softly, he swirled his tongue around and around, amazed that he was here, that she was giving him this miracle. She pulled back, and he cried out. Quickly she leaned down and finished taking off her pants, then she helped him remove his. Of course, she'd been right. Being naked was exactly what he wanted. He needed to see her bare flesh, her wonderful curves.

He got caught by the swell of her hip, and he had to kiss her right there. Then there was her stomach, so pale and smooth and lovely that he took his time exploring with his hands and his lips and his tongue.

She moved her legs slightly apart, and he was drawn to the soft golden curls at the juncture of her thighs. There would be no choice soon. He'd have to do something to ease the ache in his loins. As much as he wanted to take all the time in the world, the problem was getting serious. He didn't want to finish before he'd begun.

But first…he needed to taste her once more.

DANI FLOATED ON A SEA of sensation. She'd suspected his gentleness and his sensuality, but the proof was so far above her expectations that she had no words, even when it was impossible to stay silent. She moaned her pleasure, and used her hands to please him back.

She'd never wanted this way. Or felt more wanted. The way he looked at her. The way he tasted her. It made her feel beautiful and sexy and wanton and innocent all at the same time.

She felt his hot breath between her legs, and she shook with anticipation. He gently moved her knees farther apart, and she grabbed the pillow from the top of the bed and grasped it so tightly she could feel her fingernails on her palms.

Then his lips touched her, his tongue tickled and

enticed her. When he dipped inside her, she lost all reason. All sense of time. She was here forever, with him taking her to the stars. Nothing in her life had prepared her for this. No one had told her it could be so wonderful. He was...magic.

As she squirmed with pleasure, she reached down and touched the back of his head. Lord, she wanted him inside her. Now. "Alex," she whispered.

He stopped. "Yes?"

"I want you."

"You have me, lover."

"No. Inside me."

"Yes?"

"Yes."

He kissed her once more, then lifted himself up. He stared at her as he climbed up the bed, and then she was looking straight into his eyes.

"I want to do everything with you," he said. "Everything two people can do."

She smiled. "I know. You're so beautiful. So sweet. I never guessed it could be so..."

"Yeah. Me, neither. But it's not over. Not even close." He moved a little, and she felt him at her core. Reaching down, she grasped him, gasping a little at his thickness, then guided him. Guided him home.

He slid into her slowly, filling her perfectly. No feeling was ever like this. Nothing else made her feel so complete. It was as if she was made for him, and he for her.

Her arms went around his back, and she felt his muscles bunch and relax as he filled her and eased back. His eyes never left hers, and she felt closer to him than any other human being in the world, now or in her past, and certainly in her future. Something special was happening here, some bond that was fusing between them. He leaned down and kissed her, so that they shared the same breath while they shared their bodies.

His rhythm changed, growing faster and more urgent. Her stomach clenched, and her excitement grew. Every movement of his rubbed her in that one spot, bringing her closer and closer to climax.

She wrapped her legs around his waist. No more thinking. Only feeling. Flying. Surging. Then her body tensed and she shattered apart in a climax that shook her to her bones.

He moaned as he felt her explosion and his thrusts became primal and fierce. The kiss was broken and she could see his face in a mask of pleasure so intense it looked like pain. Every one of his muscles tensed, and then he came, too. She was still trembling, not recovered, and this sent her over the edge once more.

When he could breathe again, when he'd captured her gaze once more, he smiled a smile that lit her up inside. "My Lord, how I love you, Dani. I want you to be mine. Forever."

She sighed deeply. "Forever," she whispered. "That's a long time."

He settled down at her side, turning her slightly with him so he didn't separate from her. She wrapped her leg over his and this fit was perfect, too.

They both still breathed heavily, and she kept having these little shuddery spasms, which made her grip him tighter still. He moaned, running his hand over her arm and her back.

"Dani?"

"Hmm?"

"I want you to come to New York."

"I know you do."

"Will you?"

She ran her fingers through his chest hair, playing with the strands idly, loving the intimacy of the simple act. "I want to," she said slowly. "I tried like hell not to want to, but I do. The thought of you leaving tears me up inside. How it happened so fast I don't know, but I can't lie to you. Well, I can't lie to myself. Not anymore."

"Thank God," he said. Then he kissed her. She fell into the kiss, knowing what she would say next might mean it was her last. When she finally pulled back, he sighed once more.

"Alex," she said, not wanting to go on. "I want to go. But I can't."

"Why not? I'll give you everything, Dani. You and Chloe will never want for anything again."

"I can't take everything you want to give. I can't. I'm not like that."

"I'm not trying to buy your love, Dani. I love you, and that's why I want to make you happy."

She studied his face intently, searching for what, she wasn't quite sure. "You love me? Honestly?"

"Yes," he said, with a certainty that made her heart skip a beat. "I know it's fast, but doesn't love happen like that sometimes?"

"I suppose so."

He touched her chin with his fingertip, making sure she looked him in the eye. "You don't feel the same, huh?"

"No. I mean, I do feel for you. More than I ever would have imagined. I'm just not so sure, that's all."

"Do you want to spend time with me?"

She nodded. "Every minute I can."

"Do you feel better when we're together than when we're apart?"

"Yes."

"Do you want to make love over and over until we're both ninety and can't do it anymore?"

She giggled. "I think it's safe to give that a big yes."

"So?"

"So, I'm not sure that's love. At least not the kind of love I want."

"Tell me. What is it you're looking for?"

"I'm not exactly sure. But I do know I don't want to be kept. Not even by you."

"Kept?"

His gaze was troubled, and she didn't like to see that. But she had to tell him the truth.

"That's a pretty old-fashioned notion," he said.

"But it's what you have in mind, isn't it?"

He didn't answer her for a long moment. His hands stilled on her back. She didn't press. He had to think this through, just as she had to.

"Have I ever told you about my father?" he asked.

She shook her head.

"You know he's a very successful man. He took the company from a nice-size enterprise to an international conglomerate. He was a genius in business, and I worshiped him since I was a boy. He taught me more than any college ever could have. His advice has made me a successful man. He tempered ambition with compassion, and he taught me to do the same. The people who worked for him stayed their whole lives. He appreciated every one of them."

"He sounds like someone I'd like," she said.

"You would. He'd like you, too. But…"

"What?"

"When I was of age, my father sat me down and gave me what he called the most important advice I'd ever hear. He said it was truly the key to his success, and that if I did nothing else in my career, only followed these rules, I'd have everything I wanted from this world."

"Wow. Those must be some rules."

Alex nodded. "They were about you."

"Me? How is that possible?"

"I didn't know at the time they were about you. He talked about women in general. My future wife in particular. My wife, and the woman I would love."

"And they're not the same person?"

"No," he said softly.

Dani tried to digest the information, but it was still too sketchy. "Go on."

"My father believed, and believed with all his heart, that the right wife was an absolute necessity."

"The right wife?"

"Yes. Just like my mother. Not the brightest woman in the world, but a world-class hostess. She was in charge of the social aspects of my father's life. And that covered a lot of ground. They entertained kings. My mother was a wonder that way. She always knew what to do in any social situation that would make her guests feel comfortable and cared for. Dad used to say she lulled them into his clutches, and I think she did just that. She decorated the house, bought his clothes, took care of every detail of his home life. He never had to worry about any of that. She was a great staff sergeant, and he always gave her full credit for her part in his success.''

''But he didn't love her.''

''No. He liked her. I know that. But he loved other women. Women who didn't know the proper etiquette for dining with a Saudi prince. Women who challenged him intellectually, but didn't interfere. He kept his business world and his private life separate.''

''Your mother was part of the business world?''

''That's right.''

Dani finally understood. He didn't see her as someone who could host a king. She was too independent to want to be a full-time hostess, caterer, shopper. He wanted her to be the other woman. The woman in his private life.

She rolled to her back, finally easing him out of her body. Suddenly she was cold. She sat up and brought her comforter up and over her. Alex, too. She didn't want to lie naked atop the bed right now.

''It didn't mean he didn't treasure his other women,'' Alex said.

''Say it, Alex. His mistresses.''

''All right. For lack of a better term. But he loved them. There weren't a whole string or anything. Just three. Long-term relationships, each one.''

''Were these women happy?''

''For the most part, yes. I didn't know them all that well. All except Helen. She's still with Dad.

They live in Switzerland now. She was my father's great love. Still is."

"Your mother?"

"She died several years ago."

"And your father still didn't marry Helen?"

"No. I don't think the rules stopped applying just because he retired."

"I see."

He brought his elbow beneath him and rested his head on his palm so he could look at her. "Do you?"

"Yes. I do understand."

"I could make you very happy, Dani. It would be a good life. One filled with love. I mean that. I'd never do anything to hurt you. It would almost be like we were married, except—"

"Except for your wife."

He opened his mouth, then shut it again. "It doesn't sound so good when you say it."

"Do you honestly expect me to say yes? To willingly go to New York knowing I'll always be the other woman? To watch you find a wife? To sit back while you share her bed night after night?"

"No. No, of course not."

"Then what are you asking me?"

He paused for a long time. "I don't know anymore."

She studied him. His brow was creased and his gaze was centered somewhere in his past.

"Didn't you ever consider that your father could have been wrong?" she asked.

"Yes," he said. "The day I met you."

"But?"

He looked at her again. The confusion in his eyes was almost painful to see. "It's not easy to change a lifetime of rules."

"I know that. I've got some rules of my own that I'm not willing to change. One of them is that I won't be your mistress."

"What if I did ask you to be my wife?"

She shook her head. "No. I'd fail you, and that wouldn't be fair. You know that as well as I do. I can't be a decoration. Or the kind of hostess you want. If I get married, it's got to be a fifty-fifty proposition."

"And love has nothing to do with it?"

"Love has everything to do with it."

"Don't you believe me? Don't you understand that I love you more than I can ever say?"

"I know you care for me. But I also know a lot more. You're out of your natural habitat, Alex. You're in a kind of limbo, I think. It's exciting and different, but you can't take this place and magically transport it to New York. It doesn't work that way."

"I don't want the place. I don't give a damn about the place. I want you."

"I'm part of this place. This is my home. My values come from being here, among these people.

My values insist that when I love, it's one hundred percent. No holding back. For a lifetime. As an equal partner.''

"Will you do something for me?"

"If I can."

"Will you think about it? Don't just dismiss it because it's not what you imagined."

"Okay. But I don't see how we're ever going to agree on this."

"I can't let this go."

"You can. So can I. But not tonight. Tonight, we can have exactly what we want." She turned to her side, and kissed him gently on the mouth. "Even if we can't have forever, I'm very grateful for right now."

He pulled her tight against him once more. "You confuse the hell out of me, you know that? You're what my father used to call a fly in the ointment."

"Sometimes," she said, rubbing her cheek on his chest, "you need a fly to remind you that the ointment needs changing."

Chapter Fifteen

The night was another restless one for Dani. Having Alex next to her in bed was more of a distraction than she'd have ever guessed. She kept wanting to touch him. To feel his skin and his hair. To press her body to his. Which of course led to things. Things that made her want to throw her values to the wind and go with him as his mistress, as his concubine, anything, as long as she was his woman.

Then they'd rest again and he'd fall asleep in her arms. She'd think about what it would be like to be Alex Bradley's mistress. The longer she thought about it, the more uncertain she became. Were her old-fashioned morals standing in the way of her one true chance at happiness?

If she let him go, would she regret it the rest of her life? So what if it wasn't traditional. She'd never let that stop her before. Hadn't she raised a child all on her own, with no help from Randy? Hadn't she gone back to school when everyone told her it was crazy? That she'd never graduate?

At about two in the morning she finally was so tired she couldn't keep from looking at the real problem. It wasn't about tradition. Or about what anyone would say. Plain and simple, she wasn't willing to share. She didn't give a damn if he'd love his wife or not. Knowing there was another woman, sleeping in his home, eating at his table, sitting on his couch, was utterly unacceptable. In Alex's world, that might seem naive and pedestrian, but she didn't care about that, either. Alex would be hers completely, or not at all. Which meant, of course, that it was not at all.

How cruel Fate was. To give her this taste of happiness, only to yank it out of her reach. But then, what had she expected? Her luck had never been good when it came to love. Alex just proved the point. There were no surprises here. Only, why the hell did he have to stop in her town? And why did making love with him feel like the best thing she'd ever done, or would ever do?

Now, with the coming of the light and the start of a new day she felt tired and sad and angry. It wasn't fair. But then, fair had never played a major role in her life. This thing between them would never work. Period. End of story. Imagining, even for a moment, that it might would only hurt her more. It was time to end the fantasy, and get back to reality.

"Morning."

She looked at Alex lying next to her. He still had

a dreamy look in his eyes that told her he wasn't really up yet, but still in twilight sleep. His smile was slow and sexy, and her insides just melted. She rose quickly and grabbed her bathrobe from the bottom of the bed. Being naked with Alex was not in her best interests.

"I caught you," he said, his voice all raspy.

"What do you mean?" she said, tying the belt snugly at her waist.

"Last night. Well, maybe it was this morning. I caught you looking at me."

"Yeah?"

"Uh-huh."

"And?"

"You wanted me," he said as he sat up. The sheet fell to his waist. Her gaze lingered on that chest of his.

"I did not," she said, forcing herself to look away. He was just too beautiful. It played havoc with her determination to put an end to this...this farce right now.

"Oh, yes, you did. It was right there, in your eyes. But there was something else, too."

"Oh?"

"Yep. Which wasn't so nice." He ran his fingers through his tousled hair, then looked at her intently. "You looked sad," he said. "Sad and confused. I didn't mean to do that to you. I wanted to make you happy."

"I know," she said, wanting to reassure him

even while she knew that would be the worst thing she could do. "But you can't always get what you want. Not even you."

"You think I might get what I need?"

"Mick Jagger might not be the sage of the ages, you know?"

Alex didn't respond. His sexy smile was gone now. "I need you," he whispered.

"No," she said. "You want me. There's a difference."

"I'm not the same man with you, Dani. I'll never be that man again. You woke me up. Made me feel. How can I go back to business deals and stock exchanges without you? I never realized how empty it was. Honestly. I figured all I needed was a change of scenery. But that wasn't it at all. It's you."

She tried to smile, even though his words were tearing her up. "Nonsense," she said, struggling to keep her voice teasing. "You'll meet Miss New York and forget all about me."

"Don't say that."

"Why not? It's true. Face it, Alex. I'm a quick fling, that's all. A little detour on the great highway of your life. We shouldn't make more of it. It just complicates things."

"No. It's not like that. You know it isn't."

Dani shifted her gaze so that she wasn't looking him in the eye. She had to say the next words, even though she knew they were all lies. And she had to make him believe her. "It's true for me, Alex."

His stillness told her she'd been convincing. She had to move now, get away from him before he said something that would make her crumple. She headed for the bathroom. "I think you'd better get up and get changed," she said. "I'd rather Chloe didn't see you in here."

She didn't wait for an answer. She just ducked inside her bathroom and closed the door. Her forehead came to rest on the cool wood. Dammit, why did this have to be so hard? If she'd been asked a few days ago if love at first sight was possible, she'd have laughed. Now, she knew that all the fairy tales about instant romance were true, except, of course, for the happy endings. She'd fallen, all right. Hard. Alex had breezed into her life and messed her up for good. Now how was she supposed to find someone who really could be part of her life? There wasn't a man alive who could compare to him. Certainly not in Carlson's Gap.

All she had to do was get through today. They'd be at the street festival, and Alex would be the center of attention. She'd be thrust into the background while the town fell at his feet. That would be a good thing. A taste of what life would be like with the Sexiest Man in the World. Today would make saying goodbye easier. At least, she hoped so.

ALEX DIDN'T WANT TO SIGN autographs. He didn't want to smile politely, answer questions or have his picture taken. If it wasn't for the fact that he was helping raise money for Dani's clinic, he would have turned around and walked away.

But this was for Dani. Maybe the only thing he could give her. So he let Brenda, in her rhinestone-studded jacket and skintight jeans, lead him through the already swelling crowd to a booth set up dead center in the middle of Main Street. His pictures, blown up from the *World* magazine, loomed all around him on shop windows, banners and even on balloons.

"You'll stand here, Alex," Brenda said. "And people will line up in back. The photographer will take one photo each. No more."

She had him standing in front of the booth. From here, he could see the local radio station remote truck, the NBC affiliate truck and a whole slew of other booths lining the street. Vendors were setting up arts and crafts, snacks and games. The morning sun was warm, yet a cool breeze kept things brisk. It looked to him as if the entire population of Carlson's Gap was out here doing something. Except for Dani. He knew she was out there somewhere. They'd walked here together, listening to Chloe's excited chatter the whole way. Each of them carried a cake, and surprisingly, all three confections had made it to the school booth without mishap. He'd been embarrassed to see that their cakes were priced way above the others, just because he'd helped bake them. But it made Chloe feel important and happy, so he'd let it go.

Dani hadn't said a word about it. But then, she'd been quiet all morning. Of course he knew why. He'd pretty much made a mess of things last night. How could he have been such an ass? Asking Dani to be his mistress while he married another woman? The idea was ludicrous. Insane. Yet, that's what he'd proposed.

It was a mystery to him that he could have accepted his father's notions for all these years without question. Maybe he hadn't wanted to think about it too much. It had always been the excuse he used not to get too close. But now that he did want to get close, he didn't know how.

"Can I get you something? Coffee?"

He'd forgotten about Brenda. He smiled at her briefly, then went back to looking for Dani. "No, that's okay."

"Are you sure?"

"Yes, thanks," he said, concentrating on her for the moment. She still seemed as nervous as when she'd first approached him. "Hey, it's going to work out fine," he said. "I'm sure we'll raise lots of money."

"Oh, yes. I think so, too. Especially after Mr. Chesterton gets here."

"Pardon me?"

"Your Mr. Chesterton. He should be arriving soon, don't you think? I'm so excited. Did you see that NBC is here? 'Entertainment Tonight' is sup-

posed to be coming, too. And maybe someone from
'E!.'"

"Ted is coming here?"

Brenda's expression turned puzzled. "Yes, of
course. I thought…"

"What is he going to be doing here, exactly?"

She stepped back a little, clearly in reaction to
his tone, but he didn't care. "He's bringing Carley
Ann Foxmoor. For publicity pictures. He said—"

"I can imagine what he said." Alex tried to gain
control of his anger. He knew just what Ted was
trying to do. Bringing Carley was a sneaky damn
thing to pull. He'd dated Miss California for several
months, and everyone had assumed that something
more would come of it. But he'd never made any
pretense of the fact that it was just dating. Nothing
else. Nothing more. Ted was bringing her here so
that he would see Dani next to Carley. So that he
would come to his senses.

"I think that's him now," Brenda said, her voice
quivery. He must have really frightened her.

"I'm sorry. It's not your fault," he said as he
followed her gaze down the street to his left. A
black limo approached. That was Ted all right.

"I'm so sorry, Mr. Bradley. I thought for sure
you knew. It was such a good idea."

"It's Alex, and don't worry. Your fund-raising
will go on as planned. Will you excuse me,
please?"

He didn't wait for her answer. He walked toward

the limo, forcing himself to keep his hands from turning into fists. Ted was a good assistant, the best he'd ever had, but this was going too far. They were going to have a little talk.

Just as the limo pulled to the side of the road and stopped, Alex spotted a familiar blond head in the crowd by the registration booth. Dani. What was she going to think when she saw Carley get out of that car? He didn't need this. Not after his own blunders last night.

The limo driver stepped out and went to the passenger door just as Dani caught sight of him. She was heading his way, Chloe in tow. There was no way to stop her, short of a running tackle. Damn.

"WHOSE CAR IS THAT?" Chloe asked.

"I don't know. It's big, though, isn't it?"

"Yeah. It's like the one Alex's friend had. Think that's him again?"

"Maybe," Dani said. Alex hadn't mentioned Ted coming back to town. But who else in Carlson's Gap would have access to a limo?

She waved at Alex, but he didn't wave back. Even from across the street she could see something was wrong. Her stomach muscles tightened and she felt a lump in her throat. This wasn't good. She wasn't sure why or how, but she knew. Something bad was afoot.

She slowed her pace, but Chloe pulled her along. Dani wanted to tell Chloe to stop. To turn around and run the other way, but she didn't. She just kept walking. It felt strangely like a procession to the gallows.

They reached Alex as the door to the limo opened. Instead of Ted, a woman stepped out. Not just a woman—an extraordinarily beautiful woman. The most gorgeous woman Dani had ever seen in her life. In a dress that showed off every curve of her very curvy body. Tall, long blond hair, perfect makeup, big breasts. A centerfold come to life.

"Alex!"

Dani watched the woman beam at Alex, rush toward him as if in slow motion and fling herself into his arms. Then her lips were on his, and Dani couldn't watch anymore. She felt the crowd around her, felt Chloe's hand in hers, tugging her closer to the car, but none of it really registered.

She was too busy trying to keep herself together. The pain she felt caught her off guard. It was too sharp, too debilitating. It was a struggle not to fall. How stupid she was! How could she have thought, even for one minute that Alex could be hers? It was clear he belonged with the tall blonde, not plain old her.

When she opened her eyes, the kiss had ended, but not the embrace. The woman's arms were around his neck, and Alex's hands were on her waist. They were talking. No, Alex was talking.

"That's Miss California."

"Carley someone, right?"

"God, she's gorgeous. I heard they were getting married. I think it was in the *Enquirer*."

Dani listened to the two women next to her. She felt hot tears in her eyes, and blinked them back. She couldn't stay. She couldn't.

"Come on, Chloe."

Chloe pulled against her. "I don't want to go yet."

"We have to leave. Now."

"Why?"

"I'll explain later."

"Oh, Mom."

Dani had to tug, but she finally got her daughter to follow her. She felt like a salmon swimming upstream as she fought her way through the burgeoning crowd. Everyone was talking about Alex and the beauty queen. No one seemed the least bit surprised to see them kissing in the middle of the street. The excitement was palpable, and it made Dani feel sick.

His words had been so lovely. Why did they all have to be lies? Hadn't she learned her lesson? Obviously not. No, it took public humiliation to do that.

"Mom, I think Alex was calling you."

"No, Chloe. I don't think so."

"Where are we going?"

"Home."

"But what about the booths? You promised I could do spin art. And get hot dogs."

"Maybe later."

"Mom!"

"What?"

"You're hurting me!"

Dani stopped. She loosened her grip immediately, ashamed that she hadn't even realized what she'd been doing. She turned and bent down so she could look Chloe in the eye. "I'm sorry, baby."

"It's okay. It wasn't bad."

"I'm not feeling too well, honey. That's why I want to go home."

"Are you feeling sick because that lady kissed Alex?"

Dani's heart sank. She must be completely transparent if even Chloe could see. For a moment, she thought about brushing off the comment, but she'd promised herself long ago that she was going to tell her daughter the truth, unless it would hurt her. "Yeah, kiddo. I'm afraid so."

"You know, he didn't kiss her back."

"What do you mean?"

"He didn't. I promise. I saw."

My God, how she wanted to believe Chloe's words. But believing was dangerous. Too dangerous. "How about we go over to that spin art booth?"

Chloe's face lit up with a smile. "You mean it?"

Dani nodded. "I've been needing a new T-shirt." She leaned forward and kissed her daughter on the forehead, then stood. She tried to figure out a way to get to the spin art booth without walking past Alex, but it would have meant going blocks and blocks out of their way. No. This was reality. This was what she'd suspected all along. It was only her foolish, dreaming heart that had led her astray. Better to face the facts, and get used to the pain in her gut. She had the feeling it was going to be there for a long, long time.

Taking Chloe's hand once more, gently, she led her daughter back toward the center of town, toward the huge mass of people surrounding Alex and his lady friend. If she couldn't avoid the scene entirely, at least she could edge her way around the periphery. She just didn't want to see.

No one noticed her, thank goodness. She hurried as quickly as she could, without pulling Chloe too roughly. But there were so many people in the way. It wasn't just local folks, either. One thing for sure, Alex was a draw. There's no way this little town celebration could have brought a crowd like this. Why not? The Sexiest Man in the World and Miss California? Her little neck of the woods hadn't seen this much excitement, ever.

"Mom, wait."

Dani stopped. "What's wrong?"

"Don't you hear that?"

"What?"

"Listen."

Dani did. She heard the murmur of the crowd. A siren somewhere off in the distance. Her name.

It was Alex. He was calling her. How did he know where she was? "Come on, Chloe."

She started walking again, this time tugging her daughter behind her.

"But he's calling you."

"I heard him. Thank you."

"Don't you want to see why?"

"I've already seen enough for one day."

"But..."

"You'll understand when you're older." Dani heard him call for her again. Then she heard another voice. Karen Stovall's.

"She's over here, Alex. By the pie toss booth."

"I see her!"

Dani didn't recognize that voice. All she did know was that she had to get out of here, fast. If only Chloe would hurry!

"Mom, they're all looking for you. Wait."

"No. Come on."

Chloe grabbed her with both hands and slammed on the brakes. Dani was jerked back, surprised at her little girl's strength. She had to stop. If only Chloe could understand how badly she needed to escape.

"Mom, look."

She followed Chloe's gaze right into the crowd. Something odd was happening. The people seemed to be part of some master plan, choreographed by an unknown director, for they moved, as one, to create a path right smack-dab in front of her. It was like watching the Red Sea part. At the end of the newly created path stood Alex Bradley.

He walked toward her. Alone.

some small light broke out in front of her. It was
like watching the bird as it grew smaller-smaller-
away, except path ahead was familiar.
He walked toward her. Alex.

Chapter Sixteen

Dani felt frozen to the spot. She couldn't run, even
though everything in her screamed to move, just go!
But she was held steady by the gaze of a man
twenty feet away.

She was aware of the crowd, even though she
couldn't move her eyes. They stared at her, at him,
their faces turning from side to side as if watching
a tennis match. The closer Alex got, the quieter
everything became.

What she couldn't figure out was what he
wanted. Why make this scene so public? Wasn't
she humiliated enough?

Oh, no. Behind Alex, the woman, Miss California. She was hurrying after him. Dani listened to
the *click, click* of her heels on the pavement. Wanting to look at her, Dani tried to shift her gaze, but
Alex was only ten feet away, and the connection
was too strong. So Carley was left to her peripheral
vision, which was enough. Even in her strange "almost there, but not quite" state Dani was over-

whelmed with how beautiful, how graceful she was. She belonged with Alex. He deserved someone like her.

Alex drew closer, and somehow Dani managed to take a step back. With that one move, she tried another, but something—no, Chloe's hands at her back—stopped her. Her own daughter wanted her to make a spectacle of herself in front of every last person she knew on earth. Dani prayed for an earthquake. For Superman to swoop down and take her away. Anything, just so she wouldn't have to hear Alex tell her goodbye.

It was too late. He stood in front of her, close enough for her to see the light flecks of gold in his dark brown eyes. To see the worry lines on his forehead. To see his beautiful full lips pressed together so tightly they appeared white.

"Why did you run off?" he asked.

She swallowed, trying to get some moisture in her mouth so she could speak. "I didn't run off," she said, her voice sounding only a little raspy. And not nearly as shaky as she thought it would.

"I called your name. You kept on going."

"You were occupied at the time."

"I didn't ask her to come here."

"Okay."

"I didn't ask her to kiss me."

"I see."

"I don't love her."

"Uh-huh."

His hands moved to her upper arms. He squeezed her firmly enough that she could feel each individual finger. His big hands. The fingers that had crept over her body with infinite tenderness. That had grabbed her own hands and held them firm while he thrust into her until she came in a glorious burst of ecstasy.

"Dani Jacobson," he said, his voice as commanding as it was intimate. "I love you. I need you."

"Don't," she said. "It can't work. You and I both know that."

"Yes, it can. It will. I want you to be my wife."

She shook her head. "Stop it, Alex. We've been over this before. Please let me go."

"I can't let you go."

She caught and held his gaze. She had to let him know she was serious. More serious than she'd ever been before. It was her life at stake here, and his. No more games. No more tricks. Just the truth. "I can't be the wife you want. And I won't be your mistress. Not now. Not ever. Now, please, let me go."

He studied her for a long time. Searching her face for what, she wasn't sure. Wavering? Indecision? Finally his hands relaxed, then fell to his side.

She'd never felt so alone in her whole life.

Just then, Carley reached his side. She pushed up against him and snaked her arm around his waist. "Is this the famous Dani?"

"Not now, Carley," Alex said, turning to face her.

Dani heard the threat in his voice, but Carley didn't, or if she did, she didn't care.

"She's sweet, Alex. I mean it. She's just darling."

"Knock it off, Carley. I told you. You shouldn't have come. I thought I'd made that clear in Los Angeles."

"Well, we all make mistakes," she said. Then she laughed, tossing her hair behind her shoulders.

Dani watched her, fascinated. She was extraordinarily pretty, and yet now that she was close, Dani could see that she didn't really look like a person. She was a living Barbie, with impossibly large breasts on such a small frame, huge eyes and a pouty mouth ripe for a Revlon ad. Each individual part was perfect, yet the whole was somehow artificial.

"Ted is the one who made the mistake," Alex said. "I'm sorry. He shouldn't have done this. I never meant us to go any further."

"Honey, you don't know what you're thinking right now. Ted told me you'd been under a lot of strain. It's only natural. So why don't we just go back to the limo and work this out. I know I can make you feel all better."

Alex sighed. He reached for Carley's arm and stepped away from her embrace. "Look, Carley," he said, his voice kinder now. And soft, too, so that not everyone straining to hear would be successful. "You're a great kid. I had a really good time with you. But I told you from the start, it wasn't going to have this kind of ending. You said that was fine with you, remember? You said you wouldn't press. That you wanted to stay single. To play the field. Right?"

She frowned. "But things have changed. I thought—"

"I know. I should have broken it off with you right away. It's my fault. I hope you can forgive me."

"I don't want to forgive you. I want you to make it up to me."

"That's not going to happen."

Carley looked at him carefully. "It's true, isn't it? Ted wasn't lying. You really do think you love little Miss Backhoe."

"Hey—"

"You've got to be kidding. She's going to look just swell sitting with Carolyn Bessette-Kennedy at the Armani shows, huh? And can't you just picture her at Lincoln Center? For God's sake, Alex, get real. You'll get bored with her in two weeks. Just as soon as the novelty wears off."

Dani couldn't stand it one more second. She turned, lifted Chloe into her arms and ran. Just ran.

ALEX HADN'T KNOWN he could be this angry and not kill someone. He wanted to strangle Carley, and

Ted, too. But he didn't. He had more important things to do. Such as make sure Dani didn't believe one word of Carley's bull.

"Go back to L.A., Carley," he said. "Just get the hell away from me."

He turned to face Dani, but she wasn't there. Looking around frantically, all he could see were strangers. Gawking, staring, frozen as if they were glued in place.

"She left," someone said.

He found the woman who'd spoken. It was Karen somebody. She'd been to Dani's. "Where?"

"I don't know." She pointed east. "She just picked up Chloe and ran."

Alex took off. Once more, the crowd parted for him, only this time, they did it a whole lot faster. He ran, desperate to find her, to comfort her. To make her believe him.

When he reached the edge of the crowd he saw her. She was standing by the cake booth, and Mimi was next to her. Chloe took Mimi's hand. He kept running, and Dani spotted him. She turned abruptly and headed toward home.

No way he was going to let her go. No way in hell.

DANI TRIED TO RUN, but she was blinded by her tears. She didn't want to trip or fall. Not now. Not when she so desperately needed to get home. She could lock the doors there and die in private.

"Dani, wait."

She didn't listen. She wouldn't. Carley had done them both a favor. She'd finally told the truth. Someone had to. The awful reality had been sitting between them since they'd met. Alex was so far out of her league she didn't even have a map to get there. Dani had never minded being a small town girl. She'd always been proud of her community and her upbringing. Now she just felt stupid.

She'd dared to dream once before, with Randy, and she'd been shot down for her pretension. But that had been in private. This time, her arrogance and her stupidity were on display for the whole world to see. She wondered if NBC had caught that little soap opera back there, and if she'd be watching her shining moment, the moment Carley had called a spade a spade, on the evening news.

She ran faster, or at least tried to. Alex caught her arm, though, and that was that. She gave in, stopping at the corner. She'd only needed five more minutes to make it to her house.

"Look at me," Alex said. His voice was gentle, and that just made her cry harder. "Come on, sweetheart. Look at me."

She lifted her gaze, sure she looked horrible with red-rimmed, puffy eyes. Oh, well, what did that matter? What did anything matter?

"I hope you didn't believe anything that idiot had to say. She's all wet, Dani. She was looking for someone with deep pockets to support her habits. It wasn't going to be me.''

Dani sniffed. ''She wasn't such an idiot.''

''What are you talking about?''

''She was only telling it like she saw it. You would get bored with me. I wouldn't fit in with your fancy friends. I'm just a small town girl, Alex. With small town values. I don't know anything about Armani, or Tiffany's or the Empire State building.''

''Honey, there aren't going to be any tests.''

''You're not looking at this realistically, Alex. We've only known each other a few days. You can't possibly predict a happy ending for us. The odds are a million to one.''

''I've made my father's fortune six times over playing odds just like these. I've never lost.''

''I'm not a commodity you can sell when it doesn't meet your expectations.''

''Sell? I told you before, I won't let you go. Ever.''

''No. I can't believe you. I can't. It's too hard. There's too much at stake.''

''All right. Let's say, just for argument's sake, that there is a chance it wouldn't work out. Isn't that the same risk everyone takes? There aren't any guarantees in life, Dani.''

''I know. But at least you want to start out with the odds in your favor.''

''They are.'' He smiled then, and her heart lifted. She didn't know why. Nothing had changed. But his face, so hopeful and full of promise, hit a chord deep inside her. Then she got it. It was his expression. The same expression she'd seen on Chloe's face when she'd discovered something new and totally wonderful. It was a child's smile. Innocent and pure.

"Dani, I can't tell you I know everything that will happen in the future. What I can do is tell you what I want and what I promise."

She winced, reality crashing in on the brief flicker of hope she'd had. "No, don't."

"Why? Tell me what it is that scares you so much."

A great rush of sadness rose inside her. So much she couldn't bear it. "How can I believe you when no man I've loved has ever told me the truth?"

He was quiet while she struggled to keep her tears at bay. One slipped through, and Alex reached over with his thumb and gently, sweetly, took that tear away. Then he leaned closer, and he kissed her tenderly on the lips. It was a kiss she'd remember always, the one she'd think of in her last moments on earth. It held every kindness, every secret, every bit of love she'd ever dared to dream of.

When he let her lips go, he moved his arms around her back and brought her close. Cradled in his embrace, she rested her head on his shoulder and he rocked her back and forth. Then she heard his whisper.

"I won't make you do anything you don't feel

is right. I won't ask you again to come live with
me in New York. But I will ask you if you'll give
me permission to move here. Not in your house,
not if you're not ready. But close. If it's time you
need, I'll gladly give it to you.''

She tried to pull back, to object, but his grip grew
stronger and he held her steady.

"Wait, please. Until I'm done."

She settled down again, although the moment he
was through she would tell him he couldn't possibly move to Carlson's Gap.

"I won't be here as much as I'd like. It'll mean
a lot of traveling, but that's okay. We can work that
out. I can get the jet down here, so it won't be so
much of a burden. I can set up the computers here,
I can do everything I need to. But mostly, I'll have
you. That's all that really matters to me. And later,
if you decide that you feel right about it, we can
maybe get married. I mean for real. The whole nine
yards. Fifty-fifty.''

"Are you done?" she whispered.

"I think so."

Now when she pulled back, he let her go. She
had to look at him. To see his eyes. To see that he
was telling her the truth. When her gaze met his,
she knew. Absolutely, unequivocally. Alex Bradley
loved her.

And she loved him right back.

All her worries vanished. For once in her life she
trusted her instincts completely. No second-

guessing, no misgivings, no fear of the risk involved. He loved her enough to move heaven and earth. She loved him enough to leave the safety of Carlson's Gap behind.

She smiled. "Aren't you supposed to be signing autographs about now?"

His brows came down and he looked at her as if she was nuts. "What?"

"I said, aren't you supposed to be signing autographs?"

"You think that's more important than this? Than us?"

She shook her head. "No. But you are helping to raise money for the pet shelter."

"I know. I'll just pay the rest. It'll get built, don't worry."

"What do you mean, the rest?"

"I pledged the balance."

"You didn't have to do that."

"I know. I wanted to."

She smiled, feeling more peace and contentment than she'd ever dreamed possible.

"What?" Alex still looked puzzled. "What is that smile about? And why are we talking about animal shelters? Didn't you hear me?"

"I heard you."

"And?"

"And I think we need to get back to town. I mean, I wouldn't want anyone to think badly of us when we're gone. I'll be coming back, you know.

To check up on the shelter, and to make sure my practice is in good hands.''

"What?"

"You keep saying that."

"You mean…?"

She nodded. Alex just stood there, looking a little goofy with his mouth open.

"Well, if you're not going to say it, then I guess I have to."

"What?"

"You gotta work on that return, sweetie."

"Tell me!"

"No. It's *ask* me."

"Wh—" He stopped. Grinned. "Pardon?"

She grinned right back at him. "Boy, for a bright guy…" She sighed dramatically, enjoying this more than she could ever say. Then, she took his hands in hers, looked into his eyes and said, "Alex Bradley, will you marry me?"

"What?"

She shook her head. "No, the correct answer to that is, yes."

He nodded. Wow, did he nod. "Yes," he said. "Yes, and yes."

"Will you promise to love me in sickness and in health? Through good times and bad? Till death do us part?"

"Yes."

She leaned close, but just before she kissed him, she whispered, "I believe you."

Epilogue

Two years later

"*Why* can't we name him Pete?"

Dani shook her head at Chloe. She might be a whiz kid at her private school in Manhattan, but sometimes she was just a ten-year-old kid with some pretty stubborn ideas. "Because we can't name the baby after the dog."

"But it was Pete who helped you meet Daddy. If it wasn't for him, we wouldn't be having the baby."

"True. But I'm sure if you give Pete a very big bone, he'll be just as tickled."

"Alex Junior is just too boring."

"Well thanks."

Dani turned at the sound of Alex's voice. She smiled up at him as he came to the dinner table. "It smells great."

"Remember the last time I made chicken here?"

She smiled. "That was a meal I'll never forget."

"I've improved since then."

"True. But I still like Annie's cooking better."

"I don't know. It's nice to be here alone. Just us." He put the chicken down on the table and surveyed the meal he'd cooked with his very own hands. "Matter of fact, I think we ought to stay here for a while."

Dani watched him take his seat. Something was up, she could tell. That tone of voice was always a dead giveaway. "What are you thinking?"

"You sound worried."

"I am."

He put his napkin in his lap, then made a point of pouring himself a large glass of water, and filling her glass and Chloe's, too. "I just think it might be nice if we had the baby here."

"But it's all planned. What about New York?"

"It'll still be there when we want to go back."

"What about the new building?"

"Ted and Donald can handle it."

"Chloe's summer school?"

He turned to his daughter. "Would you be brokenhearted if you just had to play and draw and help Mom with the baby?"

She shook her head. "I didn't want to go to that dumb computer school anyway."

Alex looked back at Dani. "See?"

"What brought this on?"

"I was at the diner this afternoon."

"Mom."

"And Aunt Laura. Uncle Steve. Caroline. Mimi…"

"All right. I get the picture." She picked up her fork and stabbed a small piece of chicken. "Are you sure it's not going to make you crazy? We haven't stayed here more than a week since we moved."

"No. It's fine. I want to be here more. I think we should plan to stay here every summer."

"What?"

"Any minute now, we'll have two kids to think of," he said. "I want them to grow up to be just like their mom. With small town values."

"But a little New York sophistication wouldn't hurt, either."

"Nope. Together, they're an unbeatable combination, don't you think?"

"I do," she said.

"Know what another great combination is?"

"What?"

"Alexander Peter Bradley."

She laughed. "Now wait a minute."

"Chloe's right. It's all his fault we're together. If he'd stayed healthy, we'd never have met."

"See, Mom?" Chloe said. "Even Daddy gets it."

Dani looked at her family. Her beautiful young daughter. Her wonderful husband. Her hand went to her stomach, so ripe with her unborn child. Even Pete, the old guy, was curled up in the corner. All was right with her world. "Okay. You win. But you two have to tell him the story when he's old enough to ask about his name."

Chloe held out her hand and Alex grabbed it. They shook like partners. Buddies. Father and daughter. And now she'd be having Alex Junior at home, surrounded by her family and her friends.

For the rest of dinner, she didn't say much. It was good just to listen to the lively discussion between Alex and Chloe about the internet, Renoir, the New York Yankees and finally dish duty. Of course she wasn't allowed to help. Her belly got in the way, they claimed. But that was all right, too.

Listening to the laughter spilling out of the kitchen, she went to the living room, right up to the bookcase. She found the large coffee table book that was right next to the potted fern. Opening the front cover, she saw the page she'd put there over two years before. She'd wanted to keep it safe. To bring it out on long lonely nights, so she would remember her little adventure. The two days she'd spent with the Sexiest Man in the World.

She lifted the magazine cover, still pristine, and held it up. He was handsomer now, of course. Sweeter.

Her two days of adventure had turned into two years of joy. He was still the Sexiest Man in the World. And she was the Luckiest Woman on Earth.

Heat up your summer this July with

Summer Lovers

This July, bestselling authors Barbara Delinsky,
Elizabeth Lowell and Anne Stuart present three
couples with pasts that threaten their future happiness.
Can they play with fire without being burned?

FIRST, BEST AND ONLY
by Barbara Delinsky

GRANITE MAN
by Elizabeth Lowell

CHAIN OF LOVE
by Anne Stuart

Available wherever Harlequin and Silhouette books
are sold.

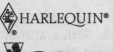

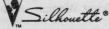

Take 2 bestselling love stories FREE

Plus get a FREE surprise gift!

Special Limited-Time Offer

Mail to Harlequin Reader Service®

3010 Walden Avenue
P.O. Box 1867
Buffalo, N.Y. 14240-1867

YES! Please send me 2 free Harlequin American Romance® novels and my free surprise gift. Then send me 4 brand-new novels every month, which I will receive months before they appear in bookstores. Bill me at the low price of $3.34 each plus 25¢ delivery and applicable sales tax, if any.* That's the complete price, and a saving of over 10% off the cover prices—quite a bargain! I understand that accepting the books and gift places me under no obligation ever to buy any books. I can always return a shipment and cancel at any time. Even if I never buy another book from Harlequin, the 2 free books and the surprise gift are mine to keep forever.

154 HEN CH7E

Name _____

(PLEASE PRINT)

Address _____ Apt. No. _____

City _____ State _____ Zip _____

This offer is limited to one order per household and not valid to present Harlequin American Romance® subscribers. *Terms and prices are subject to change without notice. Sales tax applicable in N.Y.

UAMER-98   ©1990 Harlequin Enterprises Limited

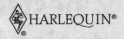

Not The Same Old Story!

Exciting, glamorous romance stories that take readers around the world.

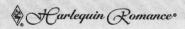

Sparkling, fresh and tender love stories that bring you pure romance.

Bold and adventurous—Temptation is strong women, bad boys, great sex!

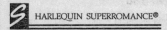

Provocative and realistic stories that celebrate life and love.

Contemporary fairy tales—where anything is possible and where dreams come true.

Heart-stopping, suspenseful adventures that combine the best of romance and mystery.

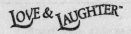

Humorous and romantic stories that capture the lighter side of love.

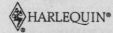 

DEBBIE MACOMBER

invites you to the

HEART OF TEXAS

Join Debbie Macomber as she brings you the lives
and loves of the folks in the ranching community
of Promise, Texas.

If you loved Midnight Sons—don't miss
Heart of Texas! A brand-new six-book series
from Debbie Macomber.

Available in February 1998
at your favorite retail store.

Heart of Texas by Debbie Macomber

Lonesome Cowboy	February '98
Texas Two-Step	March '98
Caroline's Child	April '98
Dr. Texas	May '98
Nell's Cowboy	June '98
Lone Star Baby	July '98

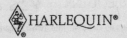

HARLEQUIN®

HPHRT1

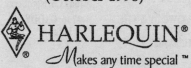

COMING NEXT MONTH

#737 DADDY BY DEFAULT by Muriel Jensen
Who's the Daddy?
When Darrick McKeon—the man she never got over—returns with twin babies, demanding if she is the mystery woman who named him as the babies' father and then disappeared, Skye Fennery knows all that stands between her and happiness is a little white lie. So she decides to *make* them a family—if only temporarily.

#738 DREAM BABY by Emily Dalton
Maggie Stern wants nothing to do with her new neighbor, the handsome yet forbidding pediatrician Jared Austin. But then a fan leaves a baby on the doorstep for the infertile character Maggie plays on TV and suddenly she has nowhere else to turn....

#739 A BACHELOR FOR THE BRIDE by Mindy Neff
The Brides of Grazer's Corners
To save her family from disaster Jordan Grazer had to go through with her wedding. But then Tanner Caldwell roared into town and whisked her away for sensuous kisses under the stars. Nothing could make Jordan go back home...except her own promise to say "I do."

#740 TUESDAY'S KNIGHT by Julie Kistler
Kally Malone had always had her life firmly in control. Not anymore! Tim's obsidian eyes and fiery kisses made her all jittery....And her daughter, Tuesday—seven going on-thirty—had a mission: to make Tim part of their family...as the daddy.

AVAILABLE THIS MONTH:

#733 AKA: MARRIAGE
Jule McBride

#734 THE COWBOY & THE SHOTGUN BRIDE
Jacqueline Diamond

#735 MY DADDY THE DUKE
Judy Christenberry

#736 DADDY 101
Jo Leigh

Look us up on-line at: http://www.romance.net